D1411451

ISLAND OF SHELLS

For John

ISLAND
OF SHELLS

BY

GRACE GREEN

MILLS & BOON LIMITED
ETON HOUSE, 18–24 PARADISE ROAD
RICHMOND, SURREY TW9 1SR

*First published in Great Britain 1993
by Mills & Boon Limited*

© Grace Green 1993

*Australian copyright 1993
Philippine copyright 1993
Large Print edition 1994*

ISBN 0 263 13775 9

*Set in Times Roman 15½ on 16 pt.
16-9405-60594 C*

*Printed and bound in Great Britain by
Mackays of Chatham PLC, Chatham, Kent*

CHAPTER ONE

A FREAK snowstorm had whirled into Vancouver during the night. Now, at eight o'clock on this Friday morning, it threw a stark white blanket over office workers making their way to the high-rise towers in the city core.

Kathryn Ashby dusted snowflakes from her blonde chignon and from her blue suede jacket as she hurried across the vestibule of the *Vancouver Clarion* building. She hadn't forgotten anything, she was sure. With the heels of her boots clicking like castanets on the snow-puddled black and white tiled floor, she mentally ticked off her check-list: passport, Air Canada tickets, camera gear, money——

The sound of laughter broke into her thoughts, just as she rounded the corner to the corridor leading to the senior editor's office. The laughter, she noted, had a distinctly malicious ring to it. With a sigh, she hitched the strap of her camera bag more securely on her shoulder and tightened her grip on the handle of her canvas weekend bag.

She thought she'd recognised the laugh, and she wasn't surprised to find that the source of the sniggering was Trish Rice. The secretary, an anorexically thin brunette, was standing at the water cooler, along with two of the junior clerks. Trish was notorious among the staff of the *Clarion* for her cattiness and gossiping, and now, as Kathryn turned the corner, she saw the other woman throw a quick, meaningful glance at her colleagues.

'Oh, hi there!' A taunting smile twisted the secretary's scarlet-glossed lips as she addressed Kathryn. 'I was just coming to look for you, to pass on the latest news ... of course, perhaps you've already heard ... ?'

Kathryn knew that Trish disliked her—the brunette seemed to resent her successful photographic career—and now, as she looked into small hazel eyes that held a smug glitter, she wondered what on earth was coming. Nothing to her advantage, of *that* she could be sure.

'Heard what?' She paused, her smile purposely vague.

Trish filled a paper cup with water from the cooler before answering, taking an obvious relish in keeping Kathryn waiting. Then, in a voice that fairly crackled with spite, she announced triumphantly, 'The Panther's back!'

Kathryn felt her smile freeze in place. Her stomach gave a quick flip-flop, and for a moment she thought the cup of black coffee which had been her breakfast half an hour before was going to be lost. 'Really?' Quickly regaining control of herself, she shrugged her shoulders in a deliberately nonchalant manner. 'I thought Rex wasn't coming back from the Middle East till next week.'

'I bumped into him yesterday afternoon. I've just been telling Sarah and Amanda I had to go to the airport after work to pick up my sister, and, lo and behold, who did I meet in the car park but the *Clarion's* own pet Panther.'

'Oh?' Kathryn glanced at her watch. 'Heavens, look at the time! If you'll excuse me, I'm in rather a —— '

'Rex told me he's feeling burned-out and he's going to take some time off,' Trish continued persistently. 'He did say, though, that he'd be coming in to the office for a while later on today.'

Later on today. As she heard the words, Kathryn felt her stomach begin to stop heaving. 'Oh, I shan't see him, then.' She kept her voice steady, hiding the relief that was flooding through her. 'I'm on my way to the airport myself.'

'Where are you going?' Trish's pouting expression was like that of a child who had been denied an expected treat. In this case, Kathryn knew, the treat was to have been present at the first meeting of herself and Rex Panther since that day in early January two months ago, the day she'd won the prestigious McGillivray Award for the most outstanding photo of the year...

The day she'd made such an absolute fool of herself.

'Charlie and I,' she said, 'are going to L'Ile des Coquilles.'

'L'Ile des Coquilles?'

'An island in the Caribbean.'

'Never heard of it!'

'Possibly because it's one of the smaller ones. Flame Cantrell has a villa there—she wants us to do an interview with her for our Saturday magazine.'

'Flame Cantrell!' Amanda, the younger of the two clerks, stared enviously at Kathryn. 'You're going to photograph her for *Weekends Wonderful*?'

Kathryn nodded. 'That's right —— '

'But she *never* gives interviews!' Trish tossed her empty cup into the rubbish bin with an irritable gesture. 'Compared to her, Greta Garbo would have won a Miss Congeniality prize! She never, never, *never* talks to the Press.'

'Tut, tut.' Kathryn shook her head reprovingly. 'Don't you know, Trish, you must never say ''never''? And I thought you were a James Bond fan!'

Sarah and Amanda tittered, and Kathryn moved past the group, the heels of her leather boots clicking smartly on the tiled floor again. As she left, she threw over her shoulder in an artificially sweet tone, 'Oh...do tell Rex how sorry I am to have missed him!'

And that, she admitted, as she strode along the corridor towards the editor's office, was a lie of the first water. If she didn't see Rex Panther again, that would be too soon for her. He was the most overbearing, obnoxious, oversexed...

She blew out an angry breath and made herself slow down. It was ridiculous, how she'd let just one kiss, one stupid, meaningless kiss, upset her so...

And why had she let it upset her?

It was two months since it had happened, but it hadn't taken her two months to come up with an answer to that question. It had taken only a few hours. Now, as she made her way to Ken's office, she frowned, finding herself going over the occasion in her mind, for what was probably the thousandth time.

The day she'd won the McGillivray Award, Ken had called her into his office during the lunch hour to break the news. No one else had seemed to know about it, or, if they had, they hadn't mentioned it to her. She had, of course, felt disappointed, but had kept her disappointment to herself. She hadn't suspected anything untoward when Ken had put a call through to her office around three, asking her to come and see him before going home, but when she'd opened his office door it had been to a loud clamour of voices shouting 'Surprise!'

All the staff were there, crammed into the small room, and they had been waiting for her. They had sent out for Chinese food, and on Ken's desk was an array of plastic glasses and several bottles of white wine.

The only person missing was Rex Panther. He was on leave and not due in the office till the following day. Kathryn was glad he was absent—for some reason she couldn't fathom, she never felt at ease with him. As the paper's foreign correspondent, he had been with the *Clarion* for almost a year—had come there from New York—but, according to Charlie Burke, her partner, who perhaps knew him better than any of the others, he was something of a mystery man—'a very private person', to use Charlie's exact words. Not that he wasn't popular with the staff—he was. But even so, Kathryn knew that he never mixed socially with any of them after work.

But after her party was over, and everyone had gone home except herself, Ken and Trish—who was on clean-up duty—the door swung open and, to her astonishment, who should have come in but Rex. Looking absolutely devastating—Kathryn felt her legs become weak as she took in his five o'clock shadow, his windswept dark hair, his tight-fitting black jeans and ancient black leather jacket—he said he'd just heard about the party and had come to congratulate her. And as she stood there, as incapable of moving as if he had cast a spell on her, he walked across and grasped her lightly by the shoulders...

And then he kissed her.

It was, she was sure, intended as just a brief, impersonal, congratulatory kiss, but somehow, when their lips met, it didn't work out that way. Sexual electricity jolted savagely between them, and Kathryn felt as if her whole body were going up in flames. His mouth was hard and possessive, his breath was warm and intimate, and his hair smelled of man and musk. He was undeniably, blood-stirringly, potently male... and it was four years since she'd been kissed. And she had never before been kissed like this! To make matters worse, her defences were at an all-time low... and the white wine she'd drunk earlier hadn't helped. She found herself yielding in his embrace, heard a faint, animal whimper in her throat. Her lips parted willingly, her body swayed into his, her fingers clung to the butter-soft fabric of his jacket...

When finally he released her, there was a strange, glazed look in his eyes, a look that belied the quirk of humour at the corners of his lips. 'Well, surprise, surprise,' he murmured, so softly that the others couldn't have heard him. 'There's a woman in there after all!'

Her response was swift and totally unpremeditated. Her right hand sliced the air, the slap she administered to his high-boned cheek angry and uncontrolled.

She heard a gasp of astonishment coming from Trish, a startled grunt from Ken. For a moment, she just stood there, hardly able to believe what she had done... and then blindly she snatched up her purse and fled from the office, leaving the door to swing shut behind her. She half walked, half ran along the corridor to her own office, scooped up her winter coat and her equipment, and, terrified she might bump into Rex again, used the fire exit stairs to leave the building and went right home.

By the following morning, she had calmed down. She had gritted her teeth, and analysed her reaction with all the honesty of which she was capable...and had come up with the only conclusion possible. She had hit out at Rex not because of the kiss but because he had hurt her. His teasing words had hurt her. But how could he have known that those words would touch on a raw nerve—those words that had implied that up till that moment of kissing he had doubted that she was a woman? During the past four years, hadn't she doubted that very thing herself...and didn't she still doubt it?

It was no wonder, then, that his softly spoken remark had hurt.

But it had been delivered in all innocence. Only a handful of people knew her secret...and Rex Panther was not one of them.

So she had acknowledged to herself that she had behaved abominably and had steeled herself to apologise to him first thing next day when she arrived at the *Clarion* building. But...he hadn't been there. Trish had passed by as she had been hovering around outside his office, and, with a knowing little smile, the brunette had been quick to tell her the Panther had left for an assignment in the Middle East.

He was back now . . . and again, it was Trish who had delivered the news. But he'd been away for two months, and Kathryn had decided during those two months that, in view of the time that had elapsed, the whole incident was best forgotten. To rake it up so many weeks after the event would only attach a greater importance to it than it warranted. She had determinedly pushed it all to the back of her mind, and hoped the matter would never come up again.

Thank goodness she was going to be leaving the city this morning! Despite herself, she felt her spirits begin to lift again. She and Charlie got along famously and she'd been looking forward so much to this trip; it would undoubtedly result in one of their very best *Weekends Wonderful*.

Ken's office was at the end of the corridor, and when she reached it she knocked on the door and waited for his gruff 'Enter!' before going in. She purposely left the door ajar in the hope that some fresh air would filter in from the corridor . . . and that some of the pungently reeking smoke from Ken's inevitable cigar would filter out.

He was just putting down the phone.

No, not putting it down. *Crashing* it down. And his face, threaded with purple veins after a lifetime of hard drinking, was today the colour of an over-ripe plum—a plum that was almost bursting through its skin.

With an oath that made Kathryn grimace, he stubbed out his cigar and gestured to the padded oak swivel chair on the opposite side of his desk. 'Sit!' he commanded.

Kathryn sat. Trying not to inhale too deeply the tainted air, she folded her hands on her lap, and patiently waited. She'd worked for Ken Webster for three years, and knew him well enough to be aware that when he was in this mood that was the only thing to do. Wait. Wait till he had calmed himself enough to speak coherently...

'*That damned Charlie*!'

'Charlie?' As Ken's fiercely spluttered words broke into her thoughts, Kathryn raised her finely arched blonde eyebrows. 'What on earth has he done now? Don't tell me he's been fiddling his expenses——'

'His whole family have come down with measles.'

'Oh, my lord!' Kathryn felt her lips twitching. Charlie Burke had three children under the age of five. Poor Emma would have her hands full for the next few days.

'What in God's name are you grinning about?'

With an effort, Kathryn compressed her lips into a straight line. 'Sorry, Ken, I was just picturing Emma with all those children lying in bed, their little faces covered in red spots——'

'Goddammit, Kate! Didn't you hear me? I said—his whole family!'

'His...*whole* family?' Kathryn stared at him. 'You mean...Charlie too? Charlie? Charlie's got measles?' she asked disbelievingly.

'Yes, dammit, the inconsiderate fool's in bed with measles. And he's supposed to be flying from here with you in——' he glanced at his watch '—just over two hours.

'*And I've got nobody else to send in his place.*'

At last, Kathryn understood why Ken was so distraught; and now she felt exactly the same way. She couldn't go to the island on her own... They needed someone to interview Flame Cantrell, needed Charlie, who had an incredible talent for drawing out even the most wary interviewee. The movie star had made it very clear that this was to be a once-in-a-lifetime feature, and had made it equally clear that every word written about her, every picture taken, had to have her approval. It was in their contract. There was just no one who could touch Charlie...

With the exception, of course, of Rex Panther. Fleetingly, Kathryn thought of all the awards lining the walls of the foreign correspondent's small office. He was, it was said by those who knew, a genius. With an impatient frown, she dismissed him firmly from her thoughts.

'What are we going to do, Ken?' Despising the childish wail in her normally self-assured voice, Kathryn looked across at the editor pleadingly. 'We can't lose this chance. We'll never get it again. We need —— '

'What we *need*,' Ken said, rolling his bloodshot eyes towards the ceiling in despair, 'is a miracle.'

'A miracle.' A deep, mocking voice came from the direction of the doorway. 'Funny, I've never thought of myself in that way... but somehow... yes, I must say I like the sound of —— '

'Panther!' Ken half heaved himself, wheezing, from his chair and then dropped down again with a thump. 'Good God, man, I wasn't expecting you till next Tuesday.'

'Wrapped things up sooner than expected and a friend of a friend got me a lift back in a private jet.' For the first time, he let his eyes rest on Kathryn. 'So... Katie, my love, we're off to L'Ile des Coquilles, are we?'

Kathryn sat there in her chair, able to do nothing but stare up at him as her heart, after its first jolting shock, began thudding again. Rex Panther—deeply tanned and fit-looking—was leaning lazily against the door-jamb, his hands bunched casually in the slash pockets of his leather jacket, his tawny eyes gleaming with amusement. He must have just come in from outside, Kathryn realised; there was a light scattering of snow on his glossy black hair—hair which, in her opinion, he always wore far too long for someone of his supposed maturity. It tended to curl distractingly over his shirt collar—more than once, as he'd passed by her office door, she'd been hit by an almost over-whelming urge to run after him, to catch be-tween her fingers the thick, curling strands, and snip them off with a pair of sharp scissors. What was it about the man that made her want to change him? Why did just looking at him irritate her so? Why did he always wear that battered-looking black leather jacket when she had no doubt that he could well afford some-thing better? Why was he still able to look so relaxed and so damned sexy when he'd just re-turned from a gruelling assignment in a country that was war-ravaged and God-forsaken? Foreign correspondents were supposed to look gaunt and hard-bitten—weren't they?—when they came back from two months in hell.

She pursed her lips. His flavescent eyes were still fixed on her, still glittering with contained laughter, as he waited for her reply.

She cleared her throat and, swivelling her chair so that her shoulder was presented to him, addressed her response to Ken.

'Surely you wouldn't ask...Rex...to take this on? Trish was just telling me she bumped into him yesterday afternoon at the airport, and he said to her that he was burned-out and was planning to take a break...'

Her protest trailed away as she heard Rex chuckle. Damn! Now he would think she had been gossiping about him with Trish, when nothing was further from the truth.

'You're right, Katie.' His voice was silky-smooth. 'I had planned to take a break.' He cocked his head towards the window as she forced herself to swivel round and face him again. 'But given a choice between taking that break here, with this freak snowstorm swirling around us, or in the Caribbean...' His smile was bland. 'Which would you choose?'

'My God, Kathryn.' Ken's frustrated voice had her swivelling back to look at him, and she saw that he was now glowering at her over the top of his half-glasses. 'Have you gone completely *daft*? I'd have thought you'd have more sense than look a gift horse in the mouth.' Wheeling back his chair, he curled his fingers around its scarred wooden arms and pushed himself to his feet. 'If *you* haven't, believe me, I have.' He turned his attention to Rex. 'Thanks,' he said tersely, 'I appreciate your offer and your next bonus will reflect that. Now, let's get this show on the road. You two get the hell out to the airport, and I'll arrange things from this end. Your ticket'll be waiting for you, Rex, at the Air Canada counter.'

'Did you bring your car to the office this morning, Kate?'

'No, I didn't,' Kathryn said stiffly. How she hated the way he called her Kate, as if she were some cute little schoolgirl. She wasn't a Kate— or, heaven forbid, a Katie! She was a Kathryn—a name that had some dignity to it— and one of these days she would make that point with Rex Panther. But now, she knew, was not the right time to go into it. 'Charlie was going to take his, and meet me here, so I took the bus...'

'Good—we won't have to squabble over which vehicle we take to the airport. Let's go, then—I'll have to drop by my place *en route* and pick up my travel bag.'

Kathryn felt a surge of annoyance at the way he had taken control. 'We don't have much time,' she began coldly, but before she could go on he said,

'My place is in Shaugnessy—just a block from South Granville Street. Won't take us a minute out of our way.' He stepped back and held the door wide open for Kathryn as she scooped up her camera equipment and her weekend bag. 'I hope you packed a bikini or two,' he murmured.

She ignored his comment. 'Goodbye, Ken,' she said, over her shoulder. 'See you next week.'

'Good luck with the interview.' The editor, now that his problems were solved, was all at once jovial. 'I have a feeling that this is going to be one of the best for *Weekends Wonderful*. If anybody can get the beautiful Flame Cantrell to open up, it'll be you, Panther.'

'I'll do my best, Ken... knowing that whatever I have to do —— ' Rex's smile held a glint of devilment '—no matter how far I have to go, or the sacrifices I may have to make to coax intimate secrets from the lovely lady, it will be for the greater good of the paper.'

Male chauvinist! Kathryn darted a scathing glance at Rex as she sailed past him... but felt her eyelids flicker as his male scent drifted fleetingly to her nostrils—male scent undiluted by any fancy designer aftershave. Though she was subjected to it for mere seconds, the brief, subtle exposure was enough to bring memories rushing into her mind with the force of a tidal wave—memories of his kiss. Though to call it a kiss was an understatement, she reflected bleakly as she tilted her chin in the air and strode off down the corridor; what it *had* been was total sensory overload. She'd had to struggle against not only his tantalising male scent and the unfamiliar feel of his rough jaw grazing her delicate skin, she'd also had to cope with the pulsing excitement that had escalated so crazily as his casual kiss had deepened swiftly, devastatingly, into something else, something wild and dark and erotic...

And more than anything, she'd had to contend with the taste of him. The taste of his lips on hers. They had been sweet, head-spinningly sweet, irresistibly beguiling and—to her great shame—totally unforgettable...

But she had to forget. Her plans for the future were all mapped out, and there was no place in them for a man. She'd tried that route and no way would she ever expose herself to the risk of that kind of hurt again...

'Here, let me carry that bag for you.'

She didn't look at Rex as he caught up with her. 'No, thank you,' she said in a cool tone, striding on briskly. 'It's not heavy. I can manage.'

'Suit yourself.' He fell into step beside her, his long legs taking one and a half strides for every two of hers. 'You don't want me to come with you, do you.' It wasn't a question, but a statement. She didn't respond.

He opened the door to the parking lot and she braced herself for the blast of frigid air that hit her face. The snow was still swirling around, and had been since dawn. She was glad she'd worn trousers and her pile-lined jacket.

'You don't like me,' he went on, and as the door swung shut behind them he cupped his hand under her elbow. She wanted to wrench her arm away, but fought the impulse. The best way to treat him was to pretend she had absolutely no feelings for him whatsoever. 'I wonder why,' he said musingly. 'Perhaps this weekend I'll find out.'

She knew his car; it was an ancient Chevelle, black and dented. It was parked close by the exit. Determinedly, she marched towards it, talking as she did. 'I can tell you now,' she said, giving him an icy glance, 'and save you some time. I find you arrogant, forward and chauvinistic.'

They reached the car and he unlocked and opened the passenger door. Taking her weekend bag from her, he tossed it into the back seat, but as she made to get in he grasped her by the upper arms. She could feel his hard fingertips digging lightly into her flesh, even through the thick lining of her jacket. With a quick, resentful frown, she looked up at him.

'You may find me all of those things,' he said, and for the first time that morning his black-lashed amber eyes held no hint of laughter, 'but there's more to it than that. Maybe you yourself don't even know the underlying reasons for your deep hostility to me.' He released her, and, the moment he did, she twitched her shoulders irritably, and, slipping away from him, lowered herself into her seat. He shut her door and she strapped herself in. By the time he got in on the driver's side, and settled himself, she was sitting staring straight ahead, her equipment on the floor at her feet, her leather purse clutched tightly in her lap. How dared he try to look inside her, analyse her?

He turned the key in the ignition. 'There's nothing I like more than a challenge,' he said softly as he pulled the car out of its parking spot and guided it towards the exit. 'You're a very intriguing woman, Kate Ashby. And there's a lot more to you than meets the eye. You look cool and unapproachable, with those haughty, aristocratic features and that silky blonde hair coiled into that elegant "don't touch me" chignon, but when we kissed——'

'Oh, I wondered how long it would be before you brought *that* up! So let's get it straight, shall we? When *you* kissed!' she snapped. 'Not when *we* kissed. As I remember it, you were the aggressor——'

'And as I remember it,' he broke in gently, 'you participated with as much passion as I did.'

'It was the wine,' she said, smoothing a tidying hand over the sleek surface of hair which needed no tidying.

'Why did you slap me, Katie?' There was no accusation in his tone. 'Was that the wine too?'

'What do you want—an apology?' Kathryn turned and glared at him, but he didn't take his eyes from the road. His profile was presented to her, in all its perfect masculine purity. She felt a strange quivering somewhere in the pit of her stomach. 'Then all right—I apologise. I'm sorry I slapped you. If you really want to know, I was ashamed afterwards, and I went to your office next morning to say so, but you'd gone.' She took in a deep breath. Somehow, having said what she had, she felt as if a load had lifted from her shoulders.

'Apology accepted.' He glanced briefly at her as he spoke, and she noticed the skin crinkling at the corners of his eyes as he smiled. 'But we still have to find out why you don't like me— the real reason, the deep, underlying reason— because I think there is one, Katie, my love.

'And I hope that this weekend we'll both discover what it is.'

His 'place', as he'd referred to it, was—surprisingly—a lovely old bungalow set among fir trees and rhododendrons, with a lawn that sloped down to the street. With its light blanket of snow, it looked like a fairy-tale cottage.

'What a charming house!' Kathryn exclaimed involuntarily as they pulled into the drive.

Rex switched off the engine. 'Want to come in for a quick coffee while I gather my things together?'

'Won't your wife be upset if you bring someone in this early in the morning?' Oh, lord, why had she said that? The words had seemed to come bubbling out by themselves. No way had she asked the question in order to find out if he was married; no, definitely not.

'I don't have a wife,' he said in a level tone as he got out. 'The place is empty.'

Kathryn refused to examine her feelings as he imparted this piece of information—and fought back a quite irrational and almost overwhelming desire to give rein to her curiosity and accept his invitation. Better by far that she keep things on a strictly impersonal basis with this disturbing man . . . and she doubted very much if she could do that once she had seen the inside of his home. It would tell her much more about him than she was prepared or willing to know. 'Thanks,' she said, 'but I'll wait here.'

'Suit yourself. I'll only be a few minutes.'

He went into the house and shut the door.

Kathryn closed her eyes—and, as she did, realised her cheeks were burning, burning with embarrassment. Why had she said anything about a wife? Why hadn't she said, as she had in the end anyway, 'Thanks, but I'll wait here'?

With a frustrated exclamation, she opened the door of the Chevelle and got out. The snow had almost stopped; there were just a few light flakes drifting down from the grey sky. Stuffing her hands into the pockets of her blue suede jacket, she strolled slowly along the pavement, and found that the cold air was pleasantly cooling on her flushed cheeks. The street was a quiet one, and there was a peaceful hush, the only sound the idling of a late-model station wagon which was parked at the kerb, further along the street, opposite a large Cape Cod house.

She had walked past about six or seven houses, and was almost at the station wagon, when the front door of the Cape Cod house opened and three children came out. The two older ones, a girl of around twelve and a boy about two years younger, were wearing brightly coloured parkas, and the third, a little girl of about three or four, was dressed in a pink and turquoise snowsuit and pink boots. She wasn't wearing a hat, and her long blonde hair danced in the wind. Behind her, closing the door, was a fair-haired woman in her thirties, dressed in an elegant crimson coat. As she locked the door, she called to the older girl, 'Melissa, honey, pull up Jessica's hood, please.'

'Sure, Mom!' the girl replied, and, crouching down beside the younger girl, she tucked the blonde hair into the hood and tied the drawstring carefully. As Kathryn watched, she saw the little girl, Jessica, look up at Melissa with a heart-melting smile, her large, thick-fringed eyes the dreamy blue of a robin's egg.

'Hurry up, Mom, we're going to be late for school!' That was the boy, calling back to his mother from beside the station wagon, in which a man, obviously his father, was warming up the engine.

'Sorry, I was on the phone.' The woman's breathless voice travelled clearly in the chill morning air as she hurried down the path. For just a second, her eyes—exactly the same dreamy blue as the little girl's—flickered absently over Kathryn, before moving away again. 'It rang just as I was coming out; it was...'

The rest of her words were muffled as she ushered the children into the vehicle. Then, thrusting herself into the front seat, she slammed the door and the station wagon pulled immediately away from the kerb and set off down the street.

A family, setting out for their day...and going eventually in all their different directions.

Kathryn felt her heart clench painfully. She would never have such a family, never be part of such a family.

Did that woman, with her three children, know how very lucky she was? When she put the older two to bed at night, did she read to them, tell them stories, listen to them talk about their day at school? When she tucked the little blonde girl in...what was her name— Jessica?—did she hug Jessica, and kiss her, and tell her how much she loved her?

Kathryn watched the station wagon disappear along the street, and then, with a heavy sigh, she turned and began walking back the way she'd come. When would this empty feeling leave her? she wondered despairingly. Would it ever? Or was she going to feel this way for the rest of her life? Was she going to have to endure this endless, aching void —— ?

'Come on, Kate!'

She had been staring blindly at the snowy pavement as she walked; now, as Rex's voice shattered her thoughts, she jerked her head up. He was standing by the Chevelle, by the passenger door, beckoning to her.

'Be right there!' she called, and quickened her pace.

Moments later, she was ensconced in the car, and Rex was reversing out of the drive. When they reached South Granville Street again, and they began the run out to the airport, he switched on the radio.

The announcer's voice reached Kathryn's ears from the stereo speakers set in the back of the car. 'And we can expect the snow to turn into rain by mid-morning. The weekend will be wet and windy, with the rain tapering off by Monday. Next week, we can look forward to milder weather...'

He snapped off the radio again, and Kathryn found herself mesmerised by his long, capable fingers, the square-cut nails, the dark hair curling on the back of his hand. She swallowed, and dragged her attention away, staring fixedly out of the window. What was it about this man that made her react the way she did? She'd never been so physically aware of anyone in her life...not even Derek, though she had been engaged to him...had almost married him.

Why was it that when she was around Rex Panther she had this frightening, panicky feeling that the shell that was her self was being threatened? Why was it that she felt she was in danger, that he would break the shell...and find there was nothing inside?

She sat back in her seat and closed her eyes.

Why did she have this awful feeling of premonition, that the coming weekend—which she had been looking forward to with such keen anticipation—was going to be an absolute disaster?

CHAPTER TWO

'HAVE you ever been to the Caribbean before?'

'No.' Kathryn glanced briefly at Rex, who was sitting beside her in Flame's private helicopter which had picked them up on their arrival at Guadeloupe International Airport. 'Almost, though—this is where we planned to come on...'

This is where we planned to come on our honeymoon. Derek and I. She took a deep breath and chided herself for being so careless. Thank heavens she'd clipped off the revealing words before they were uttered—she'd been so caught up in the breathtaking beauty of the scene below her that she'd been caught off guard. The less Rex Panther knew about her private life, the better pleased she'd be.

But he'd picked up on her slip. 'We?' He drawled the question lazily.

She made a great play of peering down through the helicopter window to the shimmering turquoise sea below, with its chain of islands scattered haphazardly like green jewels from a broken necklace. 'A...friend and I.'

Her tone made it clear she wasn't interested in discussing that friend.

'A man.' Rex adjusted his position slightly.

As he did, Kathryn was made intensely aware of the pressure of his arm against her own. To move away from him was impossible, as she was in the window seat, and when she had sat down in the first place she'd purposely squished herself as far from him as she could. Their flight to Guadeloupe had taken much longer than scheduled, because when they'd changed planes at Montreal's Dorval Airport a bomb scare had delayed their departure for several hours. She'd been tired by the time they set off on the second lap of their journey, and had soon drifted off to sleep...only to find, upon awakening in the early hours of the morning, that she'd been using Rex's shoulder as a pillow. Her stiff, embarrassed apology had been met with a teasing, 'No problem, Kate—it was a pleasure to have spent the night with you.'

Spent the night indeed! Anyone listening to him would have thought they'd been making mad passionate love all the way from Montreal to Guadeloupe. She'd glared at him, but, despite her indignation, couldn't help noticing how ruggedly appealing he'd looked with his unshaven jaw so darkly bristled. She'd had to fight a sudden breathless urge to cup that firm jaw in her hand, find out just how rough those stubbles would feel against the soft skin of her fingertips and palm ——

'Who was he?' Rex's voice brought her back to reality.

'Just someone I knew.' She turned now and looked at him, her eyes glacial. 'He's not in my life any more. All right?'

'Ah.' He nodded his head, as if what she said had explained something to him. 'Do you want to talk about it?'

Kathryn stared at him incredulously. 'Talk about it? With you? Whatever for?'

He shrugged. 'I'm interested. How long is it since the breakup?'

'It happened over four years ago, but ——'

'Where is he now? Is he...still around?'

'No,' she snapped. 'As far as I know, he's in California. He works with some movie company ——'

'An actor?'

'A cameraman.' Kathryn took in a deep breath. 'Look, I don't want to talk about it ——'

'So he was the one who broke it off.' The sympathy in his voice was a velvety caress. 'The wounds still raw, are they, Katie? Sorry, I didn't mean to rub salt ——'

'Oh, my,' she interrupted as the helicopter began its descent, 'we're going down. That must be L'Ile des Coquilles.' She hoped the hard brightness in her tone would let him know, once and for all, that the matter was closed. Forcing her attention away from him, she made herself concentrate on the small island as they began their descent. It was shaped like a crescent moon, its eastern side ragged from repeated poundings by the wild Atlantic swell and the easterly trade winds, its sheltered inner shores lined by a bleached white beach, and fringed with palm trees.

'That,' Rex leaned across her, his thick black hair brushing her cheek, 'must be the Cantrell homestead.'

She drew back, disturbed by his closeness, but he seemed unaware of her jerky movement. Nodding down towards the red roof of a sprawling villa at the southern tip of the crescent, on a promontory, he murmured, 'It seems to be the only large house on the island. It certainly has the best location!'

The musky scent from his hair teased her nostrils, and Kathryn felt her nerves quiver.

'If you'll excuse me,' she said in a thin voice, 'I'll just gather up my things.' She turned her head to glare at him, and found his face just two inches away from hers. His tawny eyes were warm...but as they looked into hers she saw them become slightly glazed.

'My God, Kate,' he murmured, his voice tinged with awe, 'what an incredibly beautiful woman you are. May I...?'

Before she could move, he had closed the space between them, and she felt his lips brush across hers. The kiss was as light as a summer breeze...and just as achingly sweet. Kathryn felt a great surge of some nameless yearning twist inside her, felt as drained and dizzy as she did after she'd given blood to the Red Cross. This, she decided as warning bells clanged in her head and she tried to recapture her breath, which had somehow become caught in her throat, was a complication she could well do without...

'You may disembark now.'

The sound of a man's voice, threaded with amusement, broke the spell that had wrapped itself around them, closing them off in a world of their own. Kathryn cleared her throat and as Rex drew back she looked up...and met the twinkling brown eyes of the dark-skinned pilot.

'Welcome to L'Ile des Coquilles,' he said with a smile.

Kathryn felt her cheeks turn warm. The helicopter had landed while she had been spinning around in orbit...and while she'd been spinning around in orbit this stranger had been looking at her, had been trespassing where no stranger should have been.

And it was all Rex Panther's fault. Anger started simmering inside her, and she directed it straight at him. Who did he think he was, stealing another kiss from her, when she least expected it? Unstrapping her seatbelt, she leaned down and fumbled at her feet for her camera equipment and weekend bag, giving herself a moment or two to calm herself before she had to face him again.

When she finally stood up, she saw that his eyes were blandly innocent, and she felt her anger start simmering again. He was holding out her suede jacket, which she'd stowed in the locker above her seat when she'd boarded.

'You won't be needing this for the next couple of days,' he said with a grin.

The pilot was still standing there, so all Kathryn said, as she took the jacket, was an airy, 'That'll be a nice change, won't it?' but as the pilot went ahead and stood at the doorway waiting for them she hissed under her breath, 'Don't do that again. Don't ever kiss me again. And don't even come into my *space* again! I don't like it. And I don't even like you.'

'Yes, it'll be a grand change, Katie, my love.' He spoke loudly, cheerily, for the benefit of the pilot . . . and as if he hadn't heard her hissed warning. 'I hope —— ' his smile rearranged his lean features into an expression that was so disarming that she felt her pulse-rate quicken despite herself '—that you and I can squeeze in a swim together some time during the weekend.'

He thought she would go swimming with *him*? Hmph! If she wanted to swim, then she would swim . . . but she would do it in her own good time . . . and certainly not when he was around. Not only did he have a nerve, he really did seem to love to organise other people. Well, she was one person who was not about to let herself be organised.

She ignored his comment, and, thanking the pilot with a taut smile as she passed him, de-scended the steps leading to the ground. Heat blazed down from the sky, and reflected up from the hot tarmac; she felt for all the world as if she'd walked into a furnace. Turning to look around, she found Rex right beside her . . . and a compactly built middle-aged man hurrying to meet them, his sandy hair flying askew in the breeze whirled up by the rotors of the helicopter as the machine began rising from the ground again.

The man shook their hands in turn. 'I'm Troy Bellows,' he shouted over the sound of the engine as he escorted them across the landing pad. 'Miss Cantrell's private secretary.'

Kathryn kept as far from Rex as she could, as the man escorted them towards a flight of narrow stairs carved deeply in the face of a jagged cliff.

'I'm pleased to welcome you to L'Ile des Coquilles in Miss Cantrell's place,' he went on, as they began their ascent. 'The housekeeper—Monique—is waiting to show you to your rooms, where you can freshen up. Breakfast will be served in about half an hour...at eight.'

Kathryn stopped short as they reached the top of the steps and she saw the stunning vista ahead. Right in front of them was a long, narrow pool, its green water glittering in the sun. Beyond it shimmered the rich turquoise waters of the Caribbean. And to her left, its impact almost taking her breath away, was Flame Cantrell's villa.

It was a long two-storey building with a white stucco façade, its doors painted lemon-yellow, the wooden shutters of each room painted in different pastel colours. The house was built in the Spanish style, with grilled balconies gracing the upper rooms, and a white wrought-iron staircase at the far end, winding up to the villa's second floor. Glossy green vines clung to the walls, a dramatic background for the colourful flowers and shrubs blossoming on the terrace below in brilliant profusion—Kathryn recognised bougainvillaea, fuchsias, red hibiscus, begonias and the exotically petalled moonflower; many of the others she had never seen before.

Inhaling deeply of the tangy, perfumed air, she found her fingers itching to open the catch of her camera case, but managed to resist the urge to take out her Nikon and begin shooting her first roll of film. That, she decided with a regretful sigh, would have to wait till their hostess gave her permission to start work.

'A sigh of longing, Katie? Wishing this little corner of paradise was yours?' Rex's voice, slightly mocking, reached her ears as he cupped a firm hand under her elbow and guided her up the steps to the veranda.

Sliding her arm deliberately from his grip, she glanced at him through the dark shade of her sunglasses. 'No,' she said with a scornful flaring of her nostrils, 'I was just wishing I could start working.'

The veranda was cobbled with sea-smoothed stones, as was the low wall around it. Kathryn's admiring gaze encompassed the many types of cactus plants flourishing with prickly abandon in large terracotta pots, and low-slung wooden furniture with comfortable cushions covered in a striped blue and white fabric, along with several deck-chairs. A glass-topped table was positioned at the centre of the seating area, and on it was a fluted antique silver vase of perfect red roses.

Elegance, Kathryn thought with a wry smile; the kind of casual elegance that only the very wealthy could attain.

'As I said, breakfast will be served at eight,' Troy reminded them. 'In the meantime I'll find Monique and she will show you to your rooms. Excuse me, please.'

As he disappeared through the arched entry into the house, Rex said to Kathryn, in a low voice that held none of the laughter that it usually did when he addressed her, 'This hostility you feel towards me, Kate—you're going to have to put it on hold while we're here. If you snap at me all the time it'll create an awkward tension in the air, and apart from the fact that we're guests in Miss Cantrell's home, we're supposed to be professionals... and a team. Do you think you can manage to put your dislike of me on the back burner?' He raked a hand through his black hair, which was being tossed over his forehead by the warm breeze from the ocean. 'Temporarily, of course.' As he spoke, his lips twitched slightly.

Kathryn bit back a sarcastic retort. This wasn't the time for cutting rejoinders; Rex, unfortunately, was right. In the circumstances, she had no choice but to put her dislike of him 'on the back burner', as he'd phrased it, but even as she acknowledged that she felt a faint flutter of apprehension. The only way she knew of to deal with this man, the only way to keep him at arm's length, was to spar with words. Flippant repartee was her defensive weapon. Without it, she realised uneasily, she might find herself at a disadvantage... and the idea was not at all appealing.

'Agreed,' she returned, somehow managing a neutral tone. 'Temporarily, of course,' she added.

'Good.' He took a step towards her and held out his hand. 'Shall we shake on that?'

After hesitating for a second, Kathryn offered her hand, which was clasped in a firm grip. The exchange was brief, Rex making no attempt to prolong it, yet the warm pressure of his flesh against her own was enough to send a tingle of sensation up her arm. As she moved back from him, she was relieved to hear approaching footsteps, and, on turning round, saw a middle-aged woman with white Afro-style hair, and skin the colour of milk chocolate, come through the archway from the villa.

'I'm Monique,' the newcomer announced with a friendly smile. 'Miss Cantrell's house-keeper. Come, I'll show you to your rooms.' She gestured towards the wrought-iron staircase at the far end of the veranda, and as she began strolling in a leisurely fashion towards it Kathryn and Rex followed her.

The hem of the servant's gaily coloured madras cotton dress floated around her sturdy calves as she walked up the staircase ahead of them, and Kathryn found herself envying its owner the garment's obvious coolness. Already the heat was making perspiration run down her own spine, causing her silk shirt to cling to her back, and her linen trousers to feel as thick and unbearably warm as if they were heavy wool. She couldn't wait to have a shower and change into one of her lighter, summery outfits.

'Miss Cantrell has put you both at this end of the villa,' Monique told them. 'Here is your room, Mr Panther.' She opened a door to her left, saying, 'Make yourself at home, if you please,' before continuing on along the cor-ridor with Kathryn right behind her.

Kathryn's room, she soon found out, was next door to Rex's, and just before she entered it she found herself glancing back along the corridor. She felt her heart give a little jump as she saw him still standing outside his room, watching her.

'I guess we should both have a shower and change,' he called. 'I'll come along and pick you up in half an hour. OK?'

'Fine,' she said, and then, throwing him a fake smile, she turned away and walked into her room.

'I hope you will like it here,' Monique said, hovering. 'If there's anything you need, at any time, please let me know. The phone is by your bed. Just dial nine.'

'Thank you, Monique.'

The moment the servant closed the door behind her, Kathryn dropped her weekend bag on the floor, and, laying her handbag and her camera gear on one of the chairs, walked across to the open French doors leading to the balcony. As she stepped outside, she saw that her room looked down on to the terrace where they'd been a few moments before. Ivy-covered trellises graced both sides of her little balcony, affording some privacy from the adjoining bedrooms. The ocean, blue-green and shimmering with heat, lay straight ahead, dotted with white-sailed yachts and windsurfers. A small cruise boat lay anchored in the harbour, and to Kathryn's right she could see the green-roofed houses of a small town clustered along the beach in the inner curve of the crescent.

She stretched her arms above her head, letting all the tension ease out of them. And then, absently, she drew from her blonde chignon the pins that held it in place, and slipped them into the pocket of her trousers. With an impatient shake of her head, she tossed her hair free, and then ran the fingers of both hands through it, lifting the silky, glossy swath from her nape and glorying in the feeling of freedom, now that it was no longer tightly confined.

She gazed dreamily out at the ocean, delighting in the incredible blue-green colour of the water. 'Beautiful,' she murmured. 'An absolutely beautiful sight.'

'Isn't it, though?'

As Kathryn heard the softly spoken words, she inhaled sharply. *Rex*. She felt her pulse quicken as she realised he must have been watching her; the tone of his voice left no doubt in her mind that his admiration hadn't been directed at the ocean ... But where the devil was he?

'Over here, Kate.'

As she heard the rustle of leaves to her left, she whirled towards the sound, but as she stared at the vine-covered trellis she could see nothing except glossy green leaves . . . though she could have sworn she heard a soft chuckle.

'Can't a lady have a little privacy?' she asked, her tone sharp with the irritation she felt. 'Who would have thought that a man like you would have to resort to being a peeping Tom —— ?'

'A man like me?' Disembodied laughter floated towards her. 'Tell me, Kate, what kind of a man you think I am.'

'Uh-uh—in the interests of maintaining a friendly relationship, I don't think that would be a very good idea.' Kathryn's tone was sweet as syrup, but with the gritty texture of syrup that had been sitting on the shelf too long. 'Now if you'll excuse me, I'm going to have that shower.'

He might have answered, but if he did, she didn't hear him. With a haughty tilt of her head, she had re-entered her bedroom, and, with a sharp click, had shut the French doors behind her.

'Oh, Charlie,' she muttered despairingly as she crossed the room, 'why in heaven's name did you have to come down with measles? And why at this particular time?' She had been looking forward to his company on this beautiful tropical island. Now she was stuck with an arrogant male chauvinist who thought he was God's gift to woman . . .

Or, at least, God's gift to *this* woman!

With a vexed exclamation, she crouched down and unlocked her bag, and began rummaging around for a pair of shorts and a light top. She had agreed to hide her dislike of him while they were here, on the island...and she really was going to try. But once their assignment was finished, and they were on their way home, she would no longer be bound by her promise. She would tell him then, in no uncertain terms, that from that moment on she wanted him to stay right out of her life.

She frowned as she shook the creases from her cream shorts and the matching scoop-neck cream top. Rex Panther had never seen her in anything but the clothes she wore to the office—tailored silk shirts, teamed with well-cut linen trousers or with one of her smart designer suits. It had been bad enough that he'd seen her with her hair down a few moments ago...but in a short time, unless she wanted to melt like butter in the sun for the rest of the day, she would have to emerge from her bedroom and endure having his lazy golden eyes roam all over her.

Damn! She got up from her crouching position and made for the bathroom door, her mouth compressed in a stubborn line. It was really ridiculous—she'd come all this way to take photos of the world-famous Flame Cantrell and, instead of concentrating her mind on this once-in-a-lifetime opportunity, all she could do was worry about the reaction Rex Panther was going to have to seeing her in a sleeveless blouse and shorts. She must be going crazy.

With a determined effort, she tried to stop thinking about him...and she almost succeeded. Did, in fact, till after she had come out of the shower, and happened to catch sight of her face in the bathroom mirror. Saw the pale oval shape with thick strands of blonde hair dripping around it, the huge sky-blue eyes, the full raspberry-pink lips...

She clutched her fluffy white bath-towel against her high breasts as she recalled Rex's words, spoken so reverently.

'My God, Kate, what an incredibly beautiful woman you are.'

Her finger trembled as she ran it over the soft flesh of her mouth...touching where his lips had touched her when he'd kissed her in the helicopter. She stared numbly into her eyes. Nobody had ever called her beautiful before. Not even Derek...

Derek.

The name of her ex-fiancé acted like a douche of iced water. Taking in a deep breath, Kathryn rubbed the back of her hand across her mouth, hard, as if she could rub away the memory of Rex's beguiling kiss. What a fool she was, to have been taken in so easily, by the oldest trick in the book: flattery.

She wasn't beautiful, never had been, and never would be. And what did Rex Panther hope to gain by saying she was? Biting her lip, she pulled another fluffy white towel from the rail beside the sink. Of course, she couldn't be sure, but she had a pretty good idea.

Adult male panthers, she knew, didn't lie in wait for their prey...they stalked it. Rex Panther was well named. Like his jungle namesake, he stalked his prey...and at the moment, it seemed, his intended prey was...herself.

Well, she'd be prey for no panther, and she hoped he would realise it soon.

She was not in the market for love—she swung away from the mirror and began vigorously towelling her hair dry—and she was certainly not in the market for sex!

But when she heard a confident rat-tat-tat on her bedroom door twenty minutes later, she could have sworn her heartbeats halted. Just for a second, but she was sure they halted nevertheless.

'Coming,' she called airily...and, though she despised herself for doing so, crossed to check her appearance again in the mirrored door of the wall-length wardrobe. Grimacing, she stared at herself. Because she jogged regularly and worked out three times a week at a fitness club, her slender figure was in perfect shape and she was very strong, but because she was so fine-boned the overall effect was one of feminine fragility—an effect that was the very last she wanted to achieve...and her hair didn't help.

Every instinct had told her to twist it up into its usual workday chignon, but she knew the sophisticated style would look ridiculous with her shorts...and she didn't want to leave it loose, after Rex Panther's recent reaction to seeing it like that. In the end, she'd compromised. She'd scraped it away from her face— but, instead of coiling it up, she'd fashioned it in a long, sleek plait. In addition, she'd put on no make-up, afraid it would just melt in the heat, and now she realised she looked like a teenager.

Sighing, she slipped on a pair of flat leather sandals, and made for the door. As she opened it, she forced her lips to shape a smile...a smile she had difficulty keeping in place when her eyes took in the man waiting for her.

Rex had changed into a navy sports shirt, a pair of taupe Bermuda shorts, and leather thongs, and though his black hair—still damp from his shower—had been only carelessly brushed back she thought she'd never seen him look more attractive. But what made his impact so very devastating wasn't only his looks, but the raw masculinity emanating from his body in powerful, sensual waves...waves that flowed over her and threatened to swamp her, as inexorably as if they'd been the waves of the ocean.

He'd been leaning with his right shoulder against the wall across from her door, his legs crossed at the ankle, his hands in his pockets, but as soon as he saw her he pushed his shoulder away from the wall and came slowly towards her. And as he walked, his gaze roamed slowly over her, just as she'd known it would...his pupils darkening, just as she'd known they would. She had never in her life felt so conscious of how she looked, so aware of the way her high, firm breasts thrust against the thin fabric of her flimsy top, so aware of the curve of her hip in the high-cut shorts, so aware of the slender length of her legs...

She was unable to move as he stopped in front of her, unable to move as he cupped her chin in one palm and stared into her eyes. He had shaved and a tantalising fragrance hung in the air between them, so faint that it was almost undetectable, but it was spicy with a vague hint of musk. Kathryn felt her senses respond, with a shudder, to the intimate, erotic scent...

'Oh, Katie, my love,' he spoke softly, 'you're so beautiful...but you're so young. I had no idea ——'

'I'm not so young.' Her protest was as breathless as if she'd just run a marathon, 'I'm twenty-six. Perhaps to someone as jaded as yourself that may seem young, but ——'

'Twenty-six?' His eyes—those yellow, feline eyes that were so strikingly flecked with orange and brown—bored into hers and, despite her determination to remain aloof from him, she felt a stirring somewhere deep inside her. 'You seem...much younger...' His voice trailed away and to her surprise she saw a frown gather between his brows. 'But your eyes... they're...so wise, so sad...'

His gaze deepened, till Kathryn felt as if someone was tugging her down into a bottomless pool.

'He really did hurt you —— ' Rex's voice held a trace of astonishment '—this man who was in your past. The pain is still there—must have been there all along—only I didn't see it because I didn't look hard enough...' His eyelids flickered, and his gaze drifted with agonising slowness to Kathryn's raspberry-pink lips, where it lingered, and the tension between them tightened till she thought it was going to snap.

She knew he was going to kiss her again. And she knew she wasn't going to be able to stop him ... unless she moved, and moved now.

With a quick jerk of her head, she released herself from the hand cupping her chin.

'My,' she said with an airiness she was far from feeling, 'who would have guessed you had such a vivid imagination? Surely that's wasted in your line of work, where you're required to report only the facts. Have you ever thought of trying something different—perhaps writing scripts for the afternoon soaps? You seem to have a natural talent for melodrama!'

He shook his head chastisingly. 'And you, Katie, my love, have a disturbing habit of becoming flippant every time I try to have a serious conversation with you. But I've met women like you before—women who use humour as a shield to protect the armour in which they've encased their emotions. Which emotions are *you* trying to protect, Kate? Are they so vulnerable that —?'

'For the life of me I can't imagine why you're pretending to be interested in my emotions. After all, we both know only too well that what you're really interested in is my body!' Kathryn curled her upper lip scornfully. 'You say you've met women like me...well, I've met men like *you*...men who refuse to accept that a woman can find all the satisfaction she wants or needs in a successful career, men who arrogantly believe that a woman's career is only a substitute for the lover she can't have—that under the trappings of every female's success is a frustrated nymphomaniac who wants nothing more than to lie back and whimper with desire and delight in the arms of any man who will have her.'

'Not any man, Kate.' Rex's lips widened in a grin. 'The *right* man.'

Kathryn made a sound of derision. '*Now* who's the one attempting to bring humour into a serious conversation?'

'I *am* serious, Kate.' Rex put an arm around her, and before she could draw back he'd pulled her against him. 'I do agree that for some women a career fulfils *all* their needs, but you're not one of those. Of that I'm certain. You're a woman just made for love...and for loving——'

'I assume by the way you're manhandling me,' she said, stiffening rigidly against his chest, 'that you think you're the right man for me! So why aren't I lying back and whimpering with delight —— ?'

'You will, Katie,' he chuckled. 'You will. When the moment is —— '

'When hell freezes over!' Kathryn wrenched herself away from him. 'That's when you'll find me lying back in your arms, whimpering with delight. And if I were you, I shouldn't hold my breath. Now —— ' her voice was taut '——it's after eight. I think we'd better get downstairs.' She moved away and began to walk along the corridor towards the exit at the end, hoping the unsteadiness of her legs wasn't apparent to Rex. 'We don't want to keep our hostess waiting.'

'You're running away, Kate.' Dammit, he was right beside her again, with his long, easy stride, and determined to have the last word. 'As you always do, when you don't want to face something you don't think you can handle.'

'Oh, I can handle *you*,' she snapped, without turning her head, 'with both hands tied behind my back. You flatter yourself, thinking I'm running away from y —— '

'Not from me, perhaps,' he interrupted gently, 'but from something. What is it, Katie? I'd like to help, if I can . . .'

She stopped abruptly at the head of the wrought-iron staircase and wheeled to face him.

'Haven't I made my message clear? Leave me alone . . . and *stop prying into my life.*'

Without waiting for a response, she brushed past him and clattered down the metal steps. She was glad of the rail and slid her hand supportingly along it as she descended; her eyes were blurred with the tears that had sprung there as she heard his offer of help, heard the kindness in his tone, the sincerity.

Reaching the foot of the steps, she ran a trembling hand over her eyes. Rex had just moments ago accused her of being emotionally vulnerable; the last thing she wanted was for him to discover just how very vulnerable she was . . .

Oh, lord, she had to get a grip on herself. In a moment she would be meeting Flame Cantrell. She desperately wished she could have had some time in which to compose herself, but she hadn't. All she could do was hope that the movie star would be so filled with her own importance that she wouldn't notice her agitation.

And with that prayer on her lips, Kathryn walked through the archway leading to the interior of the house.

CHAPTER THREE

'MISS CANTRELL will be down in a few minutes.' Monique placed a steaming carafe in the centre of the dining-table as she addressed Rex and Kathryn. 'In the meantime, do help yourself to coffee.' Humming contentedly, she left the dining-room, her sandals making a flip-flopping sound on the white travertine floor.

Kathryn could feel Rex's penetrating eyes on her, and to avoid them she turned her head slightly and looked around the room. The ceiling was very high, with whitewashed exposed rafters, and two fans whirling lazily, moving the breezes drifting in through louvred windows and an open French door leading to the veranda. From outside came the mellow sound of wooden wind chimes, and bird-song.

And from close at hand came Rex's voice.

'Would you like some coffee?'

She forced herself to look at him. 'Yes,' she said. 'Thanks.'

She drank hers black, but she noticed that he ladled three spoonfuls of sugar into his before adding cream. She also noticed, as she had in the car the day before, the lean beauty of his fingers and the faint scattering of dark hair on the back of his hands.

He leaned back in his chair. 'You've been hurt and you've decided to devote the rest of your life to your career. To being the best at what you do.'

His words weren't spoken in a questioning tone; they were statements of fact. What he believed to be fact. Kathryn decided to make no comment.

'Surely you're old enough—you're certainly smart enough—to know there are more fish in the sea, Kate. Surely you know —— '

'What I know —— ' she looked angrily at him over the rim of her coffee-cup '—is that I told you already this line of discussion was closed.'

'—that there's more to life than work.' He went on as if she hadn't spoken. 'There's family —— '

'I have a perfectly fine family, thank you,' she returned. 'I have a father and mother back East who adore me, and a sister too, whom I consider my best friend.'

'—and children.' Again he went on as if he hadn't heard her. 'Children, Katie, dear. You're a prickly one, there's no denying it, but I do believe that the very thing to get rid of those thorns would be...'

She wanted to close her ears but she couldn't. Somehow she had known where his conversation was leading, and yet she hadn't had time to brace herself for his words. Words which bounced back and forth inside her, echoing hollowly in the emptiness of her soul. Like arrows shot carelessly into a dark forest, with the marksman unaware that any creature had been wounded, Rex's words had brought quick, sharp pain in a place no one could see. Pain and sorrow. Dear God... she realised he was still talking.

'No room in your life for children, Kate? They have no place in your plans for the future?'

Before answering, Kathryn drank the rest of her coffee. Taking her time. Playing for time. Wanting to make sure that when she spoke her tone would give nothing away. Wanting to make sure that once she'd said her piece he'd realise the matter was closed, once and for all.

She placed her cup carefully in its saucer, and it didn't rattle.

'That's right,' she said, and could scarcely believe she sounded so calm. Calm and casual... and firm. 'My career is all that's important to me. I shall never have children.'

He shook his head. 'Now, that really surprises me. What do you have against kids, Kate ... against babies, for Pete's sake?'

'Babies?' She swallowed back the lump that was trying to close her throat and made a derisive little sound. 'They cry a lot, and they keep their parents up all night. They throw up, and they need changing every hour on the hour. And as if that weren't bad enough ... they eventually turn into teenagers!' She shrugged, as if to rest her case.

Before Rex could respond, steps sounded in the outer hallway. The click of high heels, sharp and determined. Kathryn rubbed her damp palms against the fabric of her shorts and threw up a silent prayer of gratitude. Whoever it was, she was thankful for the interruption—though she'd have been even more thankful had it come a little earlier. Rubbing the fingers of one hand over the taut muscles at her nape, she turned in her chair to face the open door, and, as she did, heard a voice she had heard many times before, though only on the soundtrack of movies. A voice that was familiar to movie-lovers the world over. A voice that was rich and sultry and more than a little affected.

The plummy voice of the beautiful English actress, Flame Cantrell, wishing them, 'Good morning, and welcome to my home.'

Kathryn didn't find it easy, but somehow she managed to push her conversation with Rex to the back of her mind as she watched the star walk towards them.

Flame Cantrell, she realised as she stared unashamedly, was even more beautiful in real life than she was on the screen. She became aware that Rex had pushed back his chair and was now on his feet; feeling an unanticipated thrill of excitement, like a star-struck movie fan, she followed his lead.

The actress—who, according to her publicity blurb, was twenty-nine—was tall and slender and voluptuous-looking. And though her flawless, creamy skin and hooded emerald eyes would have turned heads everywhere, her most dramatic asset was her extraordinary hair. A flame-coloured riot of natural curls tumbling in an electrical mass around her heart-shaped face and over her shoulders, it seemed to have a life of its own, almost sparking with energy at every small movement of her head. Kathryn felt her breath hiss out slowly; the woman was a photographer's dream. Those eyes, that hair, that almost translucent skin...

All at once, she realised the star was offering her a hand in greeting, her gold and cream cotton caftan fluttering around her figure as she moved. Gulping, Kathryn took the proffered hand, and to her amazement found the slender fingers were as cold as ice.

'Miss Ashby.' The sensual voice seemed to pulse through the air—along with the tantalising exotic French perfume she was wearing. 'I've seen your work...and I'm impressed.'

Kathryn opened her mouth to respond, but before she had the chance the hooded green eyes switched their attention to Rex.

'Mr Panther, your editor called yesterday, and informed me that you'd be taking Mr Burke's place. I have no problem with *that* and I trust we'll work well together. But, if it had been Miss Ashby who had been unable to come, I'm afraid I should have had to cancel the session.'

Ken had told Kathryn that Flame Cantrell had asked specifically for her, and when Kathryn had asked him if he knew why all he could tell her was that the star had heard of her through the publicity surrounding her photographer's award in January.

'I can understand that, Miss Cantrell.' Rex glanced at Kathryn, and said, simply, 'Kate's one of the best.'

Kathryn felt her cheeks turn warm. There was no doubting the ring of sincerity in his words. In a voice that seemed to come out of nowhere, she found herself saying, 'Rex is a genius,' and, as she saw his look of blank astonishment, felt her cheeks become as bright as the red hibiscus blossom on the buffet table.

Flame Cantrell seemed unaware of her embarrassment. 'So...a mutual admiration society,' she said in a matter-of-fact tone. 'Good—things always work out better when people get along...and since we're going to be all three spending time together this weekend I think we can dispense with formalities. Please call me Flame. Now ——' she rang a brass bell that was sitting at the end of the buffet '—let's eat. And by the way...anything we discuss over our meal will be off the record. Agreed?'

As Kathryn and Rex murmured their assent, she nodded. 'Good.' There was a flash of white gold as she pushed back the sleeve of her caftan and glanced at her watch. 'I'm expecting a...friend...to arrive shortly. After we've eaten, I'll introduce you to...' She broke off and her cinnamon-painted lips twisted in a smile—a strangely sly smile, Kathryn thought, and inexplicably felt a shiver run down her spine. There was something about the expression in Flame's emerald-green eyes as she'd looked under her lashes at Kathryn—for it was at Kathryn she'd been looking when she spoke, not at Rex—something which made her feel oddly uneasy. It had been there for only a flash—a look that had seemed cold, watchful, calculating.

Kathryn frowned and blinked, and when she opened her eyes again Flame was no longer looking at her, but at Rex, and the oddly disturbing expression was gone.

If indeed it had ever existed. Heavens, Kathryn chastised herself, she was being absolutely ridiculous—Flame Cantrell had specifically requested that she be the photographer on this assignment. Why on earth would she be looking at her in a way that was even remotely unfriendly?

'But no,' the actress was saying, and as Kathryn listened she forced herself to banish all her foolish imaginings, 'I won't tell you the identity of my friend—at least, not yet. Let it be a surprise.' Her eyes were bright and mischievous, as if, Kathryn mused, she had decided to play some harmless joke on her guests. 'Afterwards, after the surprise, we'll get to work. What I decided we'd do first, Rex—that is, if Kate doesn't mind——'

'Excuse me.' Kathryn grimaced apologetically. 'I...my name isn't Kate. It's Kathryn.'

'But I thought...' Flame raised her eyebrows, and glanced at Rex, whose face was the picture of innocence, and then back at Kathryn again. 'Oh. Kathryn. Fine.'

As she spoke, Monique came into the dining-room, pushing a trolley bearing steaming platters of bacon, eggs, sausages and pan-cakes, and with a sweeping gesture Flame said to her guests, 'Do sit down again. Monique, bring a fresh pot of coffee, please.'

Once they were all seated, and the coffee had been served, Flame said vaguely, 'Now...where was I? Oh, yes...Rex, I'd like for us to spend the morning together. You won't mind, will you, Kathryn? I'll have a private session with you later—probably in the afternoon.'

Rex glanced at Kate.

'That sounds fine by me,' she murmured. 'I'd like an opportunity to take some pictures down on the beach.'

'Good, then that's settled.' Flame sipped from her coffee-cup.

'This is a delightful island.' Rex sat back in his chair. 'How long have you lived here, Flame?'

'I bought the villa five years ago—just after I finished filming *Triangle in Paradise* on Martinique. I fell in love with the Caribbean. Of course, I have a flat in London, and a place in L.A., but I wanted somewhere...in be-tween...and this fitted the bill perfectly.' Flame took a triangle of toast from the silver toast-rack, and spread it with a thin layer of butter as she went on, 'In the future, I plan to make fewer films—I've been offered some wonderful parts lately, and fortunately I can pick and choose——'

She broke off sharply and tilted her head, as if listening. Kathryn noticed her green eyes widen, her creamy cheeks become washed with pale peach. And then she heard it, what Flame had obviously heard—the increasingly loud sound of an approaching helicopter.

The actress put down her toast and pushed back her chair. With a slightly agitated gesture, she wove her long fingers through her cascading red hair.

'Excuse me, won't you?' she murmured vaguely. 'My guest, I believe, has arrived.'

Over her shoulder, as she hurried on her high heels towards the door, she called back in a floating sort of voice, 'Enjoy your breakfast. I'll...we'll...join you in a short while.'

Kathryn had been toying with a piece of melon. Now she put down her fork, and, involuntarily, glanced across the table at Rex, her eyes questioning.

'Problems in paradise?' His voice was a low murmur.

Kathryn looked back at him, not knowing what to say.

Flame had appeared perfectly relaxed till she heard the sound of the helicopter. The helicopter that was purportedly bringing her guest. Who was this person she wanted them to meet? And why was the prospect seemingly upsetting to her?

Kathryn picked up her fork again, and stuck the tines firmly into the small chunk of melon. It was really none of her business; she was here only to take pictures. Rex, on the other hand, had every right to be intrigued; his job was to learn as much as he could about the life of Flame Cantrell. Something was going on, under the surface—*that* was certain. And despite herself, she couldn't help wondering if Rex would find out what it was before they left the island tomorrow.

When Flame returned half an hour later, they were out on the veranda, Kathryn perched on the low wall, Rex standing close by.

Rex was the one who had suggested they go out into the morning sun and finish their coffee on the veranda, and Kathryn had gone along with the idea. Somehow, their shared curiosity as to why Flame had seemed agitated had—for the moment, at least—given them a common bond, and once outside, with the warmth of the sun seeping into her bones, Kathryn felt herself loosening up. Despite herself, she felt some of her hostility towards Rex begin to ebb away. Perhaps it wouldn't be so bad, she mused wryly, to spend a couple of days here with him. Granted he wasn't the comfortable, easy partner that Charlie was, but neither was he moody and unpredictable like Ken. He was good-natured, he had a sense of humour... and, of course, there was no denying he was an extremely attractive man.

She peeked up at him from beneath her lashes as she took a sip of her coffee. Gorgeous, actually. In her younger years, she'd always had a weakness for rangy men with dark hair and lean features, men who were good at their job and whose self-confident walk and demeanour announced to the world that they were proud of their achievements...

Derek had walked like that.

She felt pain slice through her. Derek, also, had been leanly built, and dark, though not nearly as tall as Rex.

And not nearly as good-looking. Rex had an inherent strength in his features that Derek had lacked... a firmness of his jaw, a ——

'Did your mother never tell you it was rude to stare?'

Rex's amused voice broke into her thoughts, and it took a second for her to refocus her eyes. When she did, she saw that he was looking down at her with a teasing smile.

'Sorry.' Damn, that stiffness was back in her voice. She sighed. 'Sorry,' she said again, forcing a smile. 'I was dreaming.'

'About...what?'

Thankfully, she didn't have to answer his question. At that moment, from behind them, from the direction of the dining-room, came the click of Flame's high heels. Along with it came a ripple of laughter, sultry and provocative. Kathryn finished her coffee, put down her cup, and stood up.

'Here we are!' Flame appeared in the doorway, and as she did her hair caught the sun and the tiny, electrical curls shimmered like a blazing russet fire. Kathryn thought she'd never seen anything so beautiful. The star paused for a moment, as if well aware of the effect she was creating, and then moved forward, her caftan billowing gently around her slender figure as the breeze played with the fabric.

Behind her, coming out from the shadowed dining-room, was the figure of a man, a man with a mass of thick, curly dark hair and a dark beard. His black T-shirt clung to his muscular body, as did his brief black shorts, revealing limbs that were hairy and deeply tanned. Flame looped an arm through one of his and led him out on to the veranda. 'Come along, darling,' she said, with a coaxing laugh, 'I have a surprise for you. A photographer and journalist from the *Vancouver Clarion* have come all the way from Canada to do a spread for their Saturday supplement, *Weekends Wonderful*. Isn't it exciting? Kathryn, Rex, I asked the man in my life to join me here this weekend, because no story about me would be complete without him—the man who was behind the camera in my last three movies, and ——'

'Derek!' Kathryn could only stare in disbelief at the familiar figure standing with Flame. It couldn't be! But it was. For a second, she hadn't recognised him because of the beard; Derek McGavin had been clean-shaven when she'd known him. But there was no mistaking that strong nose and those wide slate-grey eyes, eyes which were looking at her now with an expression of astonishment and dismay.

'What the hell . . . ?' A vein throbbed at his temple as he turned abruptly towards Flame. 'Flame, for God's sake——' his tone was pleading '—why did you bring Kathryn here? I've told you time and time again . . .' He shook his head, as if words had failed him at this point.

Kathryn had the strangest sensation that she was fading away, that she was going to disappear. Her breath exhaled in a trembling sigh, and vaguely she felt Rex's arm go around her, supporting her.

Flame had crossed her arms in front of herself, and was plucking at the fabric of her sleeves with restless fingers. Her green eyes darted from Rex and Kathryn back to Derek. 'Don't be annoyed with me, darling... I just wanted the best for this spread, and Kathryn, apparently, is the best—she did, after all, win the McGillivray Award this year. You yourself were the one who pointed it out to me.'

To Kathryn's horror, a tiny sound of protest escaped her throat—a sound which Rex must have heard, because she felt the arm that was around her waist tighten.

'Would someone,' he demanded, 'please tell me what the hell's going on here?'

In a strained voice, Flame introduced the two men.

No sooner had the introductions been carried out than Rex said to Derek tersely, 'You and Kathryn obviously know each other from somewhere?'

Before Derek could respond, Flame made a dismissing gesture with one hand, the cinnamon-tipped nails making a flash of colour in

the air. 'Derek and Kathryn were once engaged, but of course that's history now. Derek
broke the engagement off four years ago, just
before he moved to Hollywood to work with
me for the first time.'

Kathryn felt a shudder run right through her;
if Rex hadn't been supporting her, she wondered if she would have keeled right over.

'Ah.' From the corner of her eye, she saw
him nod his head. 'I see.'

'I'm sorry.' Flame made a great show of
trying to sound sincere, but though it might
have fooled the others it didn't fool Kathryn;
she had no difficulty in detecting the malicious
undertone to her words. With an effort she kept
her facial expression under control as Flame
continued, 'I never dreamt it would upset you,
Kathryn, to see Derek again—but I did think
you would appreciate having a scoop for your
paper. Derek and I, you see, have kept our
affair secret till now, but the time has come for
us to let the world know we're in love . . . and
planning to get married.'

Kathryn felt as if she were stumbling through
a maze. Surely Flame hadn't brought her here
just so she could gloat over her forthcoming
marriage to Derek, knowing Derek and she had
once been engaged? It was too bizarre; what
could be her motivation? To humiliate her? To

reopen all the old wounds so that the pain would begin gouging away at her again? But why? The actress didn't even know her, so why would she want to hurt her? But even as she tried to sort out the muddle in her head, she heard Rex say, his voice seeming to come through a mist,

'So the engagement was broken four years ago?' He gave a light laugh. 'Then Kathryn must have come straight from Derek's bed to mine.' As Kathryn felt herself reeling from his words, he brushed a kiss across the top of her head. 'Whatever Kate felt about Derek has been over for a long, long time, Flame, so your apologies are quite unnecessary.' His fingertips dug into the flesh of her hip. 'Isn't that right, my love?'

Saving face. That was what it was all about, Kathryn realised as she tried to gather herself together. Rex was giving her an opportunity to preserve her self-esteem in front of these two people, and avoid humiliation. And as she remembered the pain she'd felt after Derek's betrayal, she felt a sudden desire to stab back at him, to wound him as he had wounded her.

She affected a rueful grimace. 'I'm sorry, Derek.' There was only the slightest threadiness in her tone, and she hoped no one would notice it. 'I guess the only thing you hurt was my pride, when you broke off our engagement. And once I realised that, I recovered overnight. Meeting Rex, of course, helped. It was...it was...'

'Love at first sight,' Rex supplied, as she hesitated.

'That's right,' she echoed. 'Love at first sight.'

The taut silence vibrating in the air was broken by the shriek of a brightly coloured bird which flew overhead and disappeared among the palms to the west of the villa.

'I think,' Derek announced as the sound faded away, 'I'm going to have a drink. Anyone else fancy a rum punch?'

Flame glanced at her watch, and her lips tightened. 'Don't you think it's a little early, darling...?'

Derek turned and wheeled away from her, marching back into the house as if he hadn't heard her. As he did, Monique came out to the terrace with a tray. She excused herself, before collecting the empty coffee-cups, but when she passed Flame on her way back into the house her employer stopped her curtly.

'Monique, there's been a slight misunderstanding. I didn't realise our two houseguests are a...couple. Please move Miss Ashby's things to Mr Panther's room.'

'Oh, no, that won't be necessary!' Kathryn's protest came swiftly, and she said a silent prayer of thanks to Rex as she heard him add,

'Kate's right, Flame; it won't be necessary for Monique to move her things to my room.'

But even as she felt herself begin to relax, she heard him go on silkily, 'Kate and I are perfectly able to do that ourselves. But thank you, anyway.'

The man was a monster! Kathryn opened her mouth to snap, 'Over my dead body!' but just at that moment she saw a tiny, suspicious frown puckering Flame's eyebrows, and she clamped her lips shut again. She was hoist with her own petard. Having gone along with Rex's claim that she'd gone straight from Derek's bed to his, she would only look hypocritical if she refused the opportunity to share Rex's bedroom.

And if she didn't share Rex's bedroom, then both Flame and Derek would surely guess that their story of being involved in a relationship was just that...a story. And she would have to spend her time here enduring the star's smug arrogance...not to mention Derek's guilty, pitying glances.

So she was going to have to share a bedroom with Rex Panther—for just this one night, thank heavens, as they were scheduled to leave the island the following afternoon.

But even though she knew she had no one to blame but herself for this predicament she was now in, she found herself seething inside—seething at the man standing with his arm around her. He had positively *jumped* at the chance to have her spend the night in his bedroom.

What did he think was going to happen when the lights went out? Did he expect that her gratitude would extend to her falling into his arms and making love with him?

If so, he was in for one almighty disappointment.

CHAPTER FOUR

'IF YOU so much as breathe a word about this when we get back to the office——' Kathryn glared at Rex, her hands on her hips, as he dropped her weekend bag on the stand at the foot of his bed 'I'll——'

'You'll what, Kate?' Rex turned to her with a smile tugging at the corners of his mouth. 'Deny it? Say I was living in a world of fantasy? But why? Would it be so bad if everyone found out we'd shared a bedroom? It might actually have a beneficial effect—for you, I mean— might raise your standing with the other women in the office. Perhaps you're not aware of it, but your nickname at the *Clarion* is——'

'Ice Woman.' Kathryn gritted out the words, and went on in contemptuous tones, 'How could I not be aware of it when Trish Rice referred to me by that name in the Christmas newsletter?'

Rex grinned. 'Right. And—forgive me if I sound arrogant—she did refer to yours truly as "our own pet Panther, our favourite jungle animal and sexy as hell to boot". Don't you think it would be one in the eye for Trish if she found out you were no Ice Woman, if she found out that you and I were lovers, and——?'

'Lovers?' Kathryn stared at him in outrage. '*Lovers*? Where on earth did you get the idea that we were going to be lovers? Just because we have to share a room doesn't——'

'Oh, Katie, Katie.' Rex shook his head in gentle chiding, the way he would have done with a beloved puppy who had just chewed his most comfortable slippers. 'Don't tell me you're not aware of the sexual attraction sparking between us. It's been there, beneath the surface, since the moment we met. I was hoping that by this time you'd have realised that your hostility towards me is really just an unconscious barrier you've erected, in an attempt to——'

'You're crazy—you know that? Absolutely crazy!' Kathryn whirled away from him, and strode across the room, out through the French doors, and on to the balcony. She gripped the top of the wrought-iron railing, and stared unseeingly at the waves creaming on the white beach below. Had the man no sensitivity at all? Had he no idea how it felt, to be in the situation she was in now, with her ex-fiancé downstairs ... and not only downstairs but all set to marry one of the world's most desirable women?

Tears pricked at the back of her eyes, and with an angry exclamation she brushed them abruptly away. Self-pity was not something she admired, and she was not about to start giving in to it now...

'Kate, I'm sorry.'

She hadn't heard Rex's steps—as always, she thought distractedly, he moved like a panther—but now she could feel his presence right behind her. She could have sworn she also felt compassion emanating from him.

'You're right,' he said. 'I guess I am a little crazy. I didn't take into account how traumatic it must have been for you—meeting Derek again. You've obviously not got over him yet.' He touched her arm, gently. 'Turn round, Katie—lovely though your hair is, and the delicate curve of your neck, I really would prefer to see your face when I'm talking to you.'

He thought he was crazy? She was the one who must be crazy! Just that one light touch on her skin had sent a shiver right through her, a shiver that had her wilting like a flower deprived of water. One moment she'd been wallowing in depression, the next—God help her!—she was aching with some strange, indefinable yearning. What was wrong with her?

She just couldn't fight the sensual attraction that this man held for her...couldn't fight the sheer animal sexuality that exuded from him and twined itself around her like an inescapable tentacle.

Feeling as if she were no longer in control of herself, she let her fingers uncurl from the wrought-iron rail, and, flexing the stiffness from them, turned round. He was so close that she could smell the coffee lingering on his breath, so close that she could see the sweat beading on his upper lip...and that, she realised, was too close for comfort. She leaned back against the railing, as if to get away from him.

'Look, Kate.' His tawny eyes were grave. 'I've been way out of line. I've been...pushing you...when you've not wanted to be pushed. Let's start over. From now on, I'll respect your desire to work together as professionals.' He held up his right hand, palm towards her. 'Scout's honour. No more passes, no more forcing my attentions on you. But I do like you, Kate, and I think, if you give yourself half a chance, you could like me too. So...how about it? Can we be...just friends?'

Just friends. As she looked up at him, Kathryn noticed how the sun glinted in his black hair, revealing a faint threading of silver at the temples, noticed how the lines fanned out from his eyes—laughter lines, noticed how his lips curved up into a smile, even though he was being serious.

Those lips. She shouldn't even be looking at them . . . but somehow she couldn't drag her gaze away. They were so beautifully shaped, so perfectly chiselled . . . so temptingly full and moist . . .

She cleared her throat.

'Yes.' She felt her heartbeats flutter in an astonishing little two-step as she looked up into warm golden eyes that were staring down at her intently. 'All right.' Her facial muscles seemed to have become paralysed, but with an effort she managed to twist her features into a smile. 'Just friends.'

For the merest fraction of a second, she saw something in his expression—regret, or disappointment . . . oh, she didn't know what it was. Anyway, whatever it was, it was gone again in a flash. He looked down at his watch, and said in a matter-of-fact voice, 'I guess we should be going back down now.' And when he looked up again, he had a casual smile on his face, a smile that reassured her that he had meant what he said: friends, but nothing more.

Then why was it that she now felt a twinge of the same emotions she thought she'd seen in his eyes a moment before... regret, disappointment? She stifled a sigh. What was the matter with her? She didn't seem to know, any more, what she wanted. She had never known herself to be so wishy-washy...

Was it because seeing Derek had thrown her off-balance?

Yes, she decided, grasping almost desperately at the excuse, that must be it.

But as she and Rex walked downstairs again, she found something Rex had said coming back into her mind. 'You've obviously not got over him yet.'

She grimaced. About that, he was wrong. She'd got over Derek a long time ago.

What she hadn't got over... what she would *never* get over... was the reason he'd ended their relationship——

'Watch your step, Kate.' Rex's warning words broke into her wretched thoughts as she stumbled.

'I'm fine,' she said in a reedy voice, catching hold of the railing.

And she *was* fine, she told herself with a fierce clamping of her jaw as they descended to the veranda together. She had succeeded in putting the past behind her, and only on rare occasions did she let herself dip down into the kind of depression she was suffering right now.

Once she got back to Vancouver, she would try her best to forget this weekend, to forget she had seen Derek again, and she would get on with her career.

That, after all, was what her life was now about. Her career ... and her independence.

It wasn't a choice that would be right for every woman, but it was the choice she had made, the choice that she'd felt she had to make.

And one that she was going to live with.

As she and Rex walked across the veranda, Flame, who had been relaxing on one of the blue and white striped loungers, rose languidly to her feet and turned to greet them.

'Let's go into the library, Rex, where it's cool.' She glanced at Kathryn. 'And you're...going to take some pictures, down on the beach, I think you said?'

'That's right.' Kathryn tried to sound friendly.

'Good. Then —— ' Flame crooked an arm through Rex's '——we'll see you back at the villa for lunch, around twelve, all right?'

It was obviously intended as a rhetorical question, for, without waiting for a response, she drew Rex away, talking to him in her plummy voice, and Kathryn was left alone.

Which suited her just fine, Kathryn decided tautly as she tightened her grasp on her camera and made for the steps leading down to the beach. Apart from the fact that she was itching to get to work, she needed some time alone to recharge her batteries, some time alone to try to capture the serenity she craved, the serenity that had seemed so bound and determined to elude her from the moment Rex Panther had turned up in Ken's office the day before.

She did, in fact, achieve a measure of serenity, for the beauty of the morning, the spectacular upward shots she got of the villa from the water's edge and her intense absorption in her work combined to see to that...but it was a serenity that was destined to be short-lived.

She, Rex and Flame met in the dining-room at noon; Derek was conspicuous by his absence, but Flame made no mention of him. Had he been drinking all morning? Kathryn couldn't help wondering. Had he perhaps passed out upstairs? But though Flame didn't offer any reason or excuse for his absence, she appeared to be distracted and vague during lunch.

When they were finished, she pushed her coffee-cup to one side, and said coolly, 'I normally have a siesta at this time.' Her hooded green gaze moved from Rex to Kathryn, where it settled. 'I suggest you do the same. It's really too hot to do anything else.'

The buffet lunch had been delicious, and, despite her restless mood, Kathryn had enjoyed it, and had eaten more than she'd intended; she'd have liked nothing more than to lie down and rest awhile. But to rest in her room—or rather their room, the room she had to share with Rex—with him resting beside her on the bed? She felt a quick surge of panic.

'I think ——' she avoided looking at Rex '—I'll take a walk down to the village.'

'The *bourg*?' Flame frowned...and then shrugged carelessly. 'As you please... I suppose you do need to take some shots there, to get a broader picture of the island. But if you go, you must take Rex with you. You mustn't wander around on your own—the crime rate here is very low, but still...'

Kathryn opened her mouth to protest, but, before she could, Flame rose to her feet and said, 'I'll have Troy drive you down.'

'Oh, that's not necessary...' She finally got the words out, but it was too late. Flame had already left the dining-room and her shoes were click-clicking across the hall.

Damn! Kathryn looked down at her lap, where her hands were twisted tightly together.

The last thing she wanted was to spend time alone with Rex...

'You would have been wise to have a siesta.' Rex's voice broke into her thoughts. 'It wasn't necessary for you to arrange to go out—you're quite welcome to have our bedroom to yourself. I'd have been happy to lounge in the shade, by the pool.'

'If you think I wanted to go to the *bourg* just to avoid being in the bedroom with you, you're quite mistaken.' Kathryn pushed back her chair and got up. She looked across at him steadily as he got to his feet too. 'Flame's right—I need to take some background pictures...'

'Why are you so jumpy, Kate?'

'Jumpy? What on earth makes you think I'm jumpy?'

'You looked like a frightened rabbit when Flame suggested we have a siesta. Does it bother you so much, having to share a bedroom with someone of the opposite sex, or —— ?'

'It doesn't bother me one iota —— '

'Or is it that you have to share the bedroom with... *me*? Don't you trust me, Kate? Or —— ' his tawny eyes were deceptively lazy as they penetrated hers '—is it yourself you don't trust?'

'Oh, my lord, the conceit of the man! Do you really think that if we're forced by circumstances to lie on the same bed I'll be unable to keep my hands off you?'

'I don't know, Kate,' he said simply. 'Will you?'

'Oh!' For a moment she couldn't find words to express her rage, but she knew that the blazing look in her eyes would let him know exactly how she felt. Drawing in a rasping breath, she said harshly, 'The fact that you and I have to share a room is a matter of complete and utter indifference to me. You say you want to be friends but you don't act like a friend. You act more like a . . . more like a psychiatrist! Well, I don't want a psychiatrist . . . and I don't need a psychiatrist. I am sick to death of your endless questions, your persistent attempts to dig into my psyche. From now on——' she curled her upper lip scornfully '——I plan to act as though you don't exist.'

Before Rex could respond, there was the sound of quick, heavy footsteps crossing the hall, and as Kathryn, her breathing still slightly ragged, turned towards the door she saw Troy coming into the dining-room.

'Miss Cantrell asked me to drive you to the *bourg*,' he said, with a worried flutter of his hands, 'but I've some correspondence I really must deal with right away.' He addressed Rex.

'Would you mind driving down yourself? The jeep is round the back.'

'No problem.' Rex turned to Kathryn. 'When would you like to leave?' His good-natured tone showed her scathing attack hadn't had the slightest effect on him.

'I'll be ready in ten minutes,' she said with a curt, dismissive movement of her shoulders.

'Good.' Rex moved lazily to catch the bunch of keys Troy tossed to him. 'I'll wait for you down here.'

If Trish Rice could see her now, Kathryn thought distraughtly as she walked up the wrought-iron staircase to her room, no way would she call her Ice Woman—Female on Fire would be more apt! She felt, in fact, as if she were burning up with a fever. Her cheeks were flushed—partly from the heat, of course, but mostly because of the effect Rex Panther was having on her ... just as he was responsible for the pooling of sweat under her breasts, the rivulets of perspiration running down her spine, the unpleasant clamminess of her hands.

He was wreaking havoc with her built-in body thermostat!

She had told him she was going to act as if he didn't exist. Oh, easy enough to *act* as if he didn't exist ... but try telling that to her emotions. With one supercilious quirk of his eyebrow, he could stimulate anger that surged though her body like a tidal wave; with one knowing glance from his golden eyes, he could provoke resentment that swept over her like red-hot lava from a raging volcano...

And with one lazy twist of his hip—lord help her—he could set off a chain reaction of excitement, sexual excitement that rocketed through her with the exhilarated abandon of a child hurtling out of school on the first day of summer.

She went into the bedroom and closed the door behind her. For a long moment she stood there, leaning back against the door, her legs as limp as two strands of overcooked spaghetti. Relentlessly, inexorably, her eyes moved to the bed.

She had managed to put off the moment she dreaded, but only temporarily. Tonight, she knew, she and Rex Panther would both be sleeping in this room. She looked around, with a sense of desperation, as she searched for some other place to lie down. There was nothing. The furniture was rattan, and though there were two cushioned chairs they held out no promise of comfort.

She drew a hand over her brow and, looking at her fingertips, saw they were wet with perspiration.

Again she looked at the bed.

It was, she noted, large. Queen-sized . . . perhaps even king-sized. It should be possible for both of them to spread out and sleep without ever touching each other.

Sighing heavily, Kathryn pushed herself from the door and made for the bathroom. Only one night, she reminded herself; it was only for one night. Surely she could get through that. There was, she was pretty sure, no danger of Rex trying to seduce her into making love—not after the contemptuous way she'd just talked to him.

So why was she feeling so panicky? Was it because he'd been right? Was she afraid she couldn't trust *herself*? Was she afraid she wouldn't be able to keep her hands off him if they were forced to sleep together?

She couldn't remember ever in her life having felt so confused and out of control before.

But then, of course, she had never before been exposed to a man like Rex Panther, a man who just needed to look at her to make her burn with resentment, a man who just needed to look at her to turn her knees to jelly.

'The first thing we have to do —— ' Rex parked the open jeep in the shade of a gigantic coconut palm at one end of the busy quay '—is get you a hat.'

They were the first words that had passed between them since their altercation in the dining-room . . . but Kathryn decided she would give him no argument; the afternoon sun had been beating down mercilessly on her head since they left the villa, and though it had taken only about ten minutes to drive down the winding, dusty track to the *bourg* she was already feeling a gentle but insistent pounding at her temples.

'I'll pick one up when I'm at the market,' she responded tautly. 'I want to take some pictures there.'

She slid out of the jeep, her camera case slung over her shoulder, along with her purse, and clicked the door shut as Rex came round to join her. Looking up at him through the tinted shade of her sunglasses, she said in an indifferent tone, 'I'll meet you back here in an hour. OK?'

His sunglasses were aviator-style, and the lenses were much darker than her own; she could see not even a glint where his eyes were . . . but there was no mistaking the spark of annoyance in his voice as he retorted, 'No, it's not OK. Flame put you in my charge—so we'll stay together, like it or not.' He added, as Kathryn opened her mouth to protest, 'You did, of course, put on sunscreen before you left the house?'

Kathryn cursed inwardly; no, she hadn't . . . and the sunscreen she'd put on that morning had, of course, been washed off during her pre-lunch shower. Rex had thrown her so off-balance that all sensible precautions had gone by the board. Wouldn't he gloat if he knew he'd had that effect on her? 'I didn't think it necessary—' her response was deliberately careless '—since we weren't going to be out for very long.'

Whatever it was he muttered under his breath wasn't complimentary, though Kathryn couldn't actually hear the words . . . but the tone was clear enough . . . as was his intention when he grasped her by one arm, and began to manoeuvre her across the street towards the noisy, bustling market at the other end of the quay.

'With fair skin like yours,' he said, pulling her to one side to avoid a group of young people chattering in French, 'you can't take any chances.'

'Has anyone ever told you you are a very controlling person?' She tilted her head up at him, defiance obvious in the slight flaring of her nostrils.

'Some people,' he said, without breaking his stride, 'need to be controlled.'

'And you're the one to do it.'

'That's right.'

Kathryn hesitated as they reached the first of a long line of stalls, her attention drawn by a display of finely carved mahogany schooners, hand-woven baskets and other native crafts, but Rex's grip tightened, and she found herself pulled along.

'First the sunscreen, and then the hat—then, if you must, some shopping.' He didn't stop till they came to a stall with an assortment of brightly coloured straw hats arranged on poles, and strung from lines of string. Only then did he release her . . . and as she glanced at the hats she heard him ask the stall owner for a tube of sunscreen. 'SPF thirty,' he specified.

She tried on a couple of the straw hats, and finally chose one in periwinkle-blue, with a wide blue and ivory cotton band. She swung it from one hand, and turned to pay for it; Rex, however, was in her way.

'Just a minute,' he said coolly. 'Let's get some of this on your face before you put on your hat.'

'I can do that myself,' she spluttered, but it was too late. He had already squeezed some of the clear gel on to his fingertips, and was now applying it to her brow. Her every instinct screamed at her to shrink back from his touch...but with an immense effort she managed to stay completely still. It would only make his gesture seem important, intimate, if she tried to avoid it; much more satisfying if she could act as if his touch had no effect on her whatsoever...

At least he couldn't see her eyes!

But even as the thought crossed her mind, he whisked off her sunglasses and stuck them in his shirt pocket. 'The nose,' he said, 'is extremely vulnerable to sunburn.'

With the tip of his index finger, he smoothed the gel carefully over her nose. The sunscreen had a crisp green scent—it crossed her mind that forever more, when she smelled that particular fragrance, she would think of this moment. She realised she had stopped breathing; she parted her lips and let the air sift gradually from her lungs...only to find her throat closing as she felt his fingertips brush across her cheeks...and then feather along her jaw...till it reached the corner of her mouth.

Up till that moment, she would have sworn there was nothing sexual about the way he was stroking the sunscreen on to her face. But now...his touch was a caress, lingering, teasing, the gel slippy on the flesh of her lower lip as he ran his fingertip over its pink fullness.

'The lips——' his voice was, she noted, as unsteady as her own heartbeats '—are especially vulnerable.'

She knew she should close her eyes so he wouldn't see that they'd become unfocused, glazed... but she couldn't; his, of course, were still concealed by his sunglasses, but her senses were alive to the erotic timbre of his voice, the seductive touch of his fingertip sliding across her lips, the faint scrape as his fingernail ran across her teeth...

Every cell in her body seemed to be swollen with desire, every cell screaming with awareness of him, every cell standing by for...

For *what*?

For Rex Panther to make love to her, in the middle of the afternoon, among the stalls in a crowded market?

'You really do have the most exquisite lips, Kate Ashby. And though I deplore some of the scathing remarks that come from between them, I find the lips themselves irresistible...'

Oh, lord, and I find you totally irresistible! The words wailed inside Kathryn's brain as she saw him begin to lower his head, saw his eyes half close, saw his lips come closer to hers. The sun was beating down on her, dazzling her, so that she felt under some kind of spell, unable to move, unable to do anything but wait, lips parted, for his kiss. His breath was sweet, his male scent head-spinningly musky, like some exotic aphrodisiac; she felt her throat turn dry, fought hard to stifle a moan...

The kiss was light, and as sweet as his breath, yet it was also a kiss that disturbed all the sleeping nerve-endings in her body. They jumped to life, yearning for more...but they were to be disappointed.

With a little sigh of regret, Rex drew back. 'Kissing you is like eating Belgian chocolates,' he murmured. 'One is never enough.'

His tone was as light as his kiss had been, yet in his eyes she saw the banked fires of desire. Dear God, she could only hope that the desire now streaming through her own body wasn't as apparent in her eyes.

The knowledge that it probably was stimulated her to move. Stepping back, she rammed the periwinkle-blue straw hat on to her head, and then, snatching her sunglasses from his pocket, put those on too. 'I think —— ' her voice was ragged '—you and I have a totally different idea as to how civilised people should behave in public!'

A low chuckle from the dark-skinned woman behind the stall made her tighten her lips. How many people had watched the intimate little scene? she wondered. And how could this man beside her act as if nothing untoward had happened, while his brief kiss had left her feeling so frustrated that she could have screamed?

'How much,' Rex was casually addressing the woman, 'for the sunscreen and the blue hat?'

As the woman replied, Kathryn saw Rex take out his wallet. She felt her frustration turn to anger, and before he could extricate any money she said in a frigid tone, 'I'm quite capable of paying for my own things, thank you.'

He jerked his head round and looked at her for a moment, as if about to argue. Then, with a little frown, he put his wallet away. 'Suit yourself,' he said, and, handing her the tube of sunscreen, wandered away.

She had been rude and ungracious, and she knew it. The realisation didn't improve her mood. Irritably she rummaged for her wallet and handed over the requisite amount, and then, walking a few yards from the stall, she spent a minute or two applying sunscreen to her arms, her nape, and the area of her chest that was exposed to the sun. Only after she'd popped the tube into her purse did she look around to see where Rex had gone. He was nowhere in sight.

Relief flickered through her. This, she decided, would be a good time to escape from him, get away on her own. Trying to look as inconspicuous as possible, she began threading her way among the crowds of tourists thronging the stalls, and had just come out from behind the trunk of a palm tree when she caught sight of him.

He was one of several people standing on the edge of the pavement, across the street, his familiar figure a dark outline against the glittering silvery blue-green of the harbour waters behind him. He was obviously looking for her...but he hadn't yet seen her...

She felt the sun burning her upper arms as she stared at him. She knew that she should slip away, knew that at any moment he might catch sight of her, but she couldn't move, couldn't drag her gaze from him...and, as she gazed, once again she felt her throat turn dry. With his tall, loose-limbed figure, his black hair, his tanned skin and his dark glasses, he was so compellingly masculine that just looking at him stimulated a physical craving that made her ache to be close to him. And she wasn't the only one affected that way, she was sure... There wasn't a woman who passed by who didn't let her gaze linger yearningly on him.

Yet it was to *her* lips that his had been pressed just moments before...

Lost in her thoughts, she didn't hear the sound of an approaching vehicle. Not until the motor scooter was yards away did she become aware of it. Wincing a little at the noise, she drew back involuntarily, and, as she did, to her horror she noticed a small child dart out from the crowd on the other side, straight into the scooter's path.

She felt a rush of adrenalin surge through her veins, but before the sight had really registered with her ... and certainly before she could have moved ... she saw a dark blur of motion as someone leaped out into the street, into the path of the scooter, and, with only a second to spare, swept the child up into his arms and safety.

The someone, she saw, was Rex.

The rescue had been effected so quickly, so smoothly, that Kathryn doubted more than half a dozen people had noticed. In a vague part of her mind, she was aware that the driver of the scooter hadn't stopped; but with a quick glance to ensure it was now safe to cross she hurried to join Rex, not even pausing to think that a moment before the only goal in her mind had been to escape.

He was holding the frightened, sobbing child in his arms. 'Hush,' he was saying in a soothing voice as she came to a halt beside them, 'it's all right. Now tell me, where can we find your mummy? Or your daddy?' He lifted his head for only a brief moment to look at Kathryn, before attending to the little boy again, smoothing his fine auburn hair back from his freckled brow.

'I don't...know,' the child hiccuped, and rubbed grubby hands over his tear-stained face. 'I got lost.' His voice once more degenerated into a pathetic wail, a wail that was interrupted as a young woman, supporting herself on a pair of crutches, suddenly materialised from the crowd, crying, 'Oh, thank God—Mikey, honey...'

The stranger, a plump redhead in a pale green sundress and huge straw hat, had one foot in a cast. After hobbling across to Rex, she supported herself on the crutches as she took possession of her son.

'How can I thank you?' she said with a grimace. 'You can't imagine what a disaster this holiday's been—first I break my foot, then hubby comes down with Montezuma's revenge, which leaves me with Mikey here, and I just can't keep up with him!' The worried lines on her plump face began to fade, and dimples appeared as she gave a rueful smile. 'But that's life, isn't it? No one ever promised it would run smoothly!' She hugged her son as she looked up gratefully at Rex. 'And thank heavens you moved so quickly. I saw it all—I was at the other side of the street and just couldn't get to him in time. I thought I was going to have heart failure!'

She turned to Kathryn. 'But if you have kids of your own, then you know the feeling. Have you any? Kids, I mean.'

'No.' Kathryn felt her skin turn cold, despite the blazing heat of the sun and the perspiration that was pooling in the small of her back. 'No, I don't have children.'

'Ah, well, you're young—plenty of time.' With a confident smile, she looked up at Rex again. 'I can tell by the way you handled Mikey here that you're fond of kids. Am I right, or am I right?'

Rex chuckled. 'Yes,' he said, 'you're right. As a matter of fact, I'm crazy about them.'

'I knew it.' The woman nodded smugly. 'That's just the kind of man you are... I've got a feeling about those things, and I'm never wrong. Well —— ' she dropped her child to the ground, and he immediately grabbed a hold of her skirt '——we'd best be getting back to our condo... and that's where we'll stay till Mikey's daddy's better. I'm not going to risk this ever happening again. Let's go, Mikey, and tell Daddy all about it.'

Empty, empty, empty.

The words echoed hollowly in Kathryn's head as the woman hobbled away, her son sticking close to her side. She herself would never know what it felt like to have a child, never know the chilling fear of losing sight of that child for a moment in the crowd, never know the heady relief at finding him—never know the comfort of being part of a threesome, bound by ties of love despite all the ups and downs of everyday living.

'Not your cup of tea, is it?'

Rex's dry comment interrupted her aching thoughts.

She turned away from him. Despite the concealing shade of her sunglasses, he might just notice the glint of tears in her eyes. Clearing her throat, she said in a voice that showed none of the emotion that was tearing at her heart, 'It would be a boring little world if we were all the same, wouldn't it?'

Perhaps she should have been an actress, she reflected bleakly, instead of a photographer; her performance was really quite convincing.

'And now, if you don't mind —— ' she took her camera out of its case and focused her attention on it '—I'd like to get some work done. That is, after all, why we're here!'

CHAPTER FIVE

DEREK was lounging alone by the pool when they got back to the villa. He looked sober enough, Kathryn decided, though a little green about the gills. He got to his feet abruptly when he saw Rex and Kathryn crossing the veranda to join him.

'Sit down,' he said with a tight smile, 'and I'll get you both something to drink. You look as if you could do with something cool—what would you like, Kathryn?'

'A tall glass of lemonade with ice would be lovely,' Kathryn replied, as she sank down on to a *chaise-longue* under the shade of a striped awning. Determined not to let him know how awkward she felt in his presence, she gazed levelly at him as she spoke, then, taking off her hat, she waved it casually in front of her like a fan for a moment or two, before placing it on the patio table at her side, along with her sunglasses. 'I'd no idea it could be so hot here!'

'Iced lemonade it is. And you, Panther? A gin and tonic, maybe?'

'Thanks, no—what Kate's having is fine with me.'

'Sure?' Derek paused in the doorway.

'Sure.' Rex crossed to the edge of the pool, and stood with his back to the sun as he went on, 'I rarely drink alcohol.'

Derek raised his eyebrows, but made no comment. With a 'Be right back' he went into the house.

Kathryn had also felt a flicker of surprise at Rex's statement. She glanced across at him, and, though he was still wearing his sunglasses, she sensed that he was looking at her. Watching her. Expecting a response? There seemed to be something of a ... challenge in his attitude.

She leaned back and affected a slow yawn before saying, 'Doesn't fit your image, somehow.'

The gentle breeze ruffled the surface of the pool, resulting in a lulling sound as the water lapped the tiled edges. 'My image?'

Kathryn lifted her shoulders in a casual shrug. 'Oh, you know what I mean—we're both aware that the image of the hard-bitten foreign correspondent, roving the world's hot spots, walking headlong into danger, and so on, is just a cliché. At least, for the most part. Don't tell me you're going to deny you spend the greater part of your time sitting around in pubs with your counterparts from other papers.'

'Why are you trying to needle me, Kate?' Sliding his hands into the pockets of his shorts, Rex took a few lazy strides and came to a halt just in front of her.

'Needle you?' She tried to ignore the way her heartbeats had lurched forward like horses from the starting gate as he approached. 'Is that what I'm trying to do?'

'What would you call it?' Under the silky tone of his voice was a thread of steel.

'An attempt to make conversation —— ' she yawned again, and gestured nonchalantly '——in a situation not of my making. For a moment, there, I forgot you weren't Charlie. Sorry—I didn't realise you were so thin-skinned. Let's talk about something else!'

She heard him hiss out a soft oath, but before he could speak she went on blithely, 'I never did ask you how your interview went this morning. Did you and Flame get off to a good start?'

He took in a deep breath, as if trying to contain his irritation with her. If that was his intention, he seemed to have succeeded, because when he spoke his voice was steady.

'No,' he said bluntly, 'we didn't. All she talked about was superficial stuff—stuff you can read in any of a dozen movie magazines in any bookstore in North America.'

'What kind of stuff?'

'The blurb her PR office gives out to anyone who cares to ask—she was born in London, England, twenty-nine years ago, only child of a travelling salesman and his stay-at-home wife. They're a close family, but her parents don't like the limelight, so she's kept them very much out of the picture. They gave her a holiday in California for a twenty-first birthday present, and she was spotted by a casting agent who was looking for a new face for the sequel to *Amber Angel*, and —— '

'And the rest,' Kathryn said, 'is history.' She sat up, and, looking at Rex, she forced herself to ignore, for the moment, the tension that always seemed to strum between them. 'Are you thinking what I'm thinking?'

He took off his sunglasses, and slid them into the breast pocket of his shirt. 'And what, curious Kate, is it that you're thinking?' His eyes were inscrutable.

She realised that he had very neatly turned the question back to herself, but it didn't seem to matter. 'That there's got to be more?' Her voice was a whisper between them. 'That it's all too...pat?'

'What we've been told...yes, that does strike me as being too pat. But,' he went on, 'it makes me think of a jigsaw puzzle which has been only partially completed. Though the finished part has been painstakingly put together, the rest of the pieces are scrambled—some may even be missing. And I suspect that *you*, somehow, fit in. I'm not sure yet where, but —— '

'Me? Surely not. I've never met Flame before today —— '

'But you were once engaged to the man she's going to marry, and it seems to me as if your presence has somehow provoked —— '

'Sorry I took so long.' Derek's voice preceded him as he came out from the house, bringing Rex's musings to an abrupt halt. Kathryn threw Rex a quick grimace, saying without words, That was a narrow escape, as Derek joined them.

'I had the devil of a job finding a lemon,' their host explained as they sat down and he served the cool-looking drinks complete with cherry, lemon, and swizzle sticks. 'It's Monique's afternoon off. She always goes to see her sister on Saturday. Oh, before I forget —— ' Derek turned to Kathryn '—Flame just phoned down from her room. She'd like you to go up there in ten minutes—she's ready for a session with you. Alone.' He hesitated, as if about to say something else, but then changed his mind, instead addressing Rex, who was just draining his glass. 'Fancy a swim to cool off, Panther?'

Rex nodded. 'Sounds like a good idea.' He got to his feet. 'I'll go up and get changed. Can I get you anything while I'm up in our room, darling? Or is there anything you'd like me to do for you?'

For about six seconds, Kathryn didn't respond. It was the 'darling' that had thrown her, of course; her mind had been wandering, and it hadn't clicked that she was the 'darling' to whom Rex was talking. But who else could it be? Certainly not Derek! Anyone less likely than Rex to address another man as darling she couldn't imagine...

So... he wanted to play the role of lover in front of Derek. Was it to convince Derek that their supposed relationship was genuine, or was he doing it just to annoy her? The latter, Kathryn decided. Well, she would show him that it didn't bother her one bit!

With a sweet smile, she looked up at him, and, trailing her fingertips along his hair-roughened forearm as he paused solicitously by her chair, murmured in a husky tone, 'Not a thing, my love, at the moment. Perhaps later...?' She let the words trail away suggestively.

She heard him make a choking sound as if he'd been caught by surprise, but when he bent to skim a light kiss across her brow, one hand sliding to cup her head as he did so, there was no mistaking the mischievous twinkle in his eyes. 'Don't promise what you don't intend to deliver, Kate!' he said, in a loud enough voice for Derek to hear...before adding in a low murmur, 'You're playing a dangerous game, my sweet.'

She felt her heart give a lurch as his lips touched the tip of her earlobe, the contact setting off an explosion of exquisitely tender sensations that danced from nerve-ending to nerve-ending across the surface of her skin. Yes, indeed, she was playing a dangerous game...and one from which she might find it difficult to extricate herself. But with Derek watching, there was no way she could withdraw from it at present, so she might as well go all the way...

'You know my opinion of people who break their promises,' she purred.

Surreptitiously Rex tweaked her plait in silent retort, and as he straightened she saw that his lips were twitching at the corners, but he said nothing more to her.

Instead he addressed Derek.

'I'll be back in a few minutes,' he told his host, and with that he moved away and went inside.

The moment he was out of earshot, Derek said, in a subdued tone, 'That remark was aimed at me, wasn't it?'

'Remark?' Kathryn frowned. 'Which remark?'

Derek scraped an embarrassed hand across his bearded jaw. ' ''You know my opinion of people who break their promises''. You aren't very subtle, Kathryn.'

Kathryn sighed. 'You're mistaken, Derek. I wasn't even thinking of you when I —— '

Derek got roughly to his feet. 'Look, I know I deserve any insults you care to throw at me, but —— '

'Stop it, Derek!' Kathryn got to her feet too and faced him. 'Take my word for it, my remark was meant for Rex, and Rex alone. Your broken promises are, as far as I'm concerned, water under the bridge.'

There must have been something in her tone that convinced him, for she saw his shoulders slump. 'Oh, God, what a mess this is. I had no idea Flame had invited you to come to the island, Kathryn. You do believe that, don't you?'

'Of course I do. It was quite obvious you were as surprised to see me as I was to see you.'

'There's something I want to explain to you ——'

'Derek, you don't owe me any explanation, OK? You and I, we went our separate ways and now we've got different lives, we're both involved with other people. I have...Rex, and you have Flame.'

'Flame.' He shook his head. 'What I feel for her—it's so different from what I felt for you, Kathryn...but that's not surprising, really, since she's so different from you. She's infuriating, unpredictable, volatile, and half the time I don't understand where she's coming from, but she's the only woman in the world for me.'

To her astonishment, Kathryn saw tears of genuine emotion glimmering in his wide-spaced grey eyes...and saw, for a fleeting moment, the man she'd fallen in love with.

He made a pleading gesture. 'Can we put the past behind us, Kathryn?'

'Oh, Derek...' Impulsively Kathryn grasped his hands and held them in a tight grip as she looked up at him. 'Yes...because that's where it belongs. And I'm truly glad you've found someone else.'

Derek's eyes were very serious. 'I thought when I first saw you again that you'd changed and become hard...but you haven't, despite...everything. It's all just a front. You're still the same sweet, loving Kathryn you always were.' He hesitated for a moment, and then tentatively leaned forward and kissed her cheek. The kiss was light, and unthreatening...and Kathryn knew it was an olive branch.

An olive branch she was quite willing to take. Though Derek had hurt her so badly, she didn't hold any festering resentment towards him as a person. He couldn't help being the kind of man he was...any more than she could help being the kind of woman *she* was. What a pity it was that they had, in the ways that really mattered, been so very wrong for each other...

'And you, Derek,' she managed a cheerful chuckle, 'are still as full of it as you always were. Now —— ' she glanced at her watch '—if you'll excuse me, I'd better get myself organised for my session with Flame.'

Turning, she happened to look up at the house...and, as she did, felt a chill shiver down her spine. She'd glanced at a window at the opposite end of the villa from the room she shared with Rex...and the face peering down at her from behind the edge of the silk curtain was Flame's.

It disappeared from view swiftly...

But not swiftly enough.

Kathryn had had ample time to see the look in the star's hooded green eyes. And it had been a look of such hostility that she had almost gasped aloud.

Had Flame been watching Derek and her talking? Had the actress seen her grasping Derek's hands and looking up so intensely into his eyes? And had the red-haired beauty seen Derek brush that fleeting kiss on her cheek?

How on earth, Kathryn wondered in dismay, was she going to get the actress to co-operate during their photographic session when she was so blatantly antagonistic towards her?

It was going to be a nightmare.

In the event, the session wasn't a nightmare after all.

It was, however, frustrating, irritating, and, Kathryn acknowledged as she strode bad-temperedly to her bedroom afterwards, totally unproductive.

She and Flame had spent almost two hours together, with the actress posing in many different outfits, and Kathryn had shot several rolls of film. But from the beginning she'd noticed a stiffness in the way Flame arranged her body, a falseness in the smile she gave for the camera. As tactfully as she could, Kathryn had tried to coax the redhead into relaxing and letting the real woman show through.

'*Sorry*, darling!' the actress had replied in a tone of deep contrition...but when, during the following shots, she'd adopted the same brittle manner and artificial smile as she had before, Kathryn had found it hard not to give vent to her exasperation. Finally, after a particularly uninspired series of shots, she had opened her mouth to plead with her subject to try for more mood, more emotion...and had suddenly detected a sly, smug glint in Flame's eyes, and, with a stab of shock, had realised that though Flame was giving every appearance of co-operating she had in fact set out to sabotage the session in a subtle but totally effective way.

What game was she playing? Kathryn had asked herself with a surge of anger, as she'd raised her Nikon to her face again and watched Flame through the camera lens. For there was no doubt she was playing a game. The movie critics were unanimous in their opinion of the famous star—it had been written so many times that it had become a cliché: the camera loved Flame Cantrell.

Every camera, of course, except Kathryn Ashby's!

Lips pursed, Kathryn stomped her way along the last few yards of the long corridor, and flung open her bedroom door with such force that it banged loudly against the wall behind before swinging shut again with a sharp click. The session, she decided as she dropped her camera gear on the nearest chair, had been a flop. A waste of time. And not only that, but insulting to her professionally.

'Flame Cantrell,' she said in a voice that positively vibrated with rage, 'is a manipulative b——'

'Tut tut!'

Kathryn froze as Rex came out of the bathroom, wearing nothing but an icy-blue towel around his waist. Another towel, a white one, was in his hands, and he rubbed it briskly through his wet hair as he grinned at her with his head at an angle. He must have spent the afternoon in the pool, and come up now for a shower, Kathryn reflected distractedly; why had it not even occurred to her that he might be up here?

Derek had played squash regularly when she'd been engaged to him, and he'd always kept himself trim and fit, but the thought came to her now that he would never have dared kick sand in Rex Panther's face. This man, she realised in one swift, breathless glance, had a figure that would have made Adonis weep with envy. Deeply tanned, with a sprinkling of black, crisp hair on his limbs and chest, it was as close to lean, hard-muscled perfection as a man could be . . .

She realised Rex was looking at her with his eyebrows quirked amusedly.

'Sorry.' She dragged her eyes from him and crossed to the French doors leading to the balcony, where she took up her stance. 'I thought you'd still be outside with Derek.'

'No need to apologise.' She could hear him giving his hair another rough massage with the towel, and then he went on lightly, 'I gather your session with her ladyship was somewhat on a par with my own.'

Kathryn found that her irritation with herself for being so susceptible to Rex seemed to further inflame her irritation with the movie star. She whirled round, feeling her cheeks burning. 'You're damned right,' she said vehemently. 'For two pins, I'd walk out right now and ——'

'And ruin your reputation . . . maybe even your career?' Rex shook his head. 'You want to be known as the photographer who walked out on an exclusive assignment with North America's hottest star?'

Kathryn knew, of course, that he was right. But that didn't make her feel any better! 'Well, do *you* have any idea what she's up to? Why bother inviting us here, if she's not prepared to co-operate?'

'Let's look at the facts.' Rex tossed the white towel over the back of a chair and moved across the room towards the bed. 'Fact number one, she was the one who asked Ken to send a team to the island. Right?'

'Right. Fact number two, according to Ken—and Flame herself—she specifically asked for me...'

'And fact number three, she didn't tell Derek she had invited you here. There was no mistaking his surprise.'

'Or his anger.'

'Anger at Flame.' Rex frowned. 'Remember what he said to her when he first saw you— "Why did you bring Kathryn here? I've told you time and time again..." Told her *what* time and time again?'

Kathryn shrugged. 'Lord knows...' Her words trailed away. To her annoyance, she realised that her attention had started straying again...straying from what she was saying...straying instead to the man she was talking to.

Rex had sat down on the edge of the bed with his legs apart, and he was leaning forward a little, his hands cupped loosely over his kneecaps...and as he spoke, restlessly and unconsciously he was beginning to slide his hands from his knees up and down his muscled thighs, the palms making a faint rustling sound as they skimmed the hair-roughened skin. And each time he slid his hands up, the lower edge of the icy-blue towel got pushed up, a little more every time, revealing more—much more—than Kathryn wanted to see.

She licked her lips, and found they were dry. 'This is getting us nowhere,' she began, but he interrupted her.

'Why would any woman who is about to get married want to bring her prospective groom into contact with his ex-fiancée?' Frowning, he scratched a hand absently across his chest, close to his left nipple, and Kathryn's gaze followed his fingertips hypnotically. The nipple was nut-brown, a shade or two darker than his tanned skin, and barely visible amid the crisp black hair curling around it.

'Kate?'

'Mmm?' Her response was jerky; she realised he was waiting for her to speak. What had his question been? 'Sorry.' She rubbed a hand distractedly across her brow, 'I . . . can't seem to concentrate . . .' Raising her head again, she met his gaze. And as their eyes locked, his became slightly glazed, as if he'd seen something in hers that had made his own thoughts begin to stray.

He got slowly to his feet. 'Kate —— ' his voice was as seductively, deceptively smooth as ten-year-old Glenlivet '——don't look at me like that unless you want me to —— '

'Sorry.' Kathryn struggled to overcome the panic screaming through her and forced herself to speak lightly as he began walking towards her. 'I didn't realise I was looking at you in any particular way. Maybe it was a trick of the light.' She moved quickly from where she was standing, saying, 'Oh, lord, isn't it hot?' and crossed to the small, built-in fridge which she knew was stocked with all kinds of soft drinks and alcoholic beverages, and pulled the door open. She stared unseeingly at the contents. 'Would you like something to drink?'

'Maybe a ginger ale.'

He was right behind her. As she reached down to get his ginger ale, and a miniature bottle of white wine and one of soda water to make a spritzer for herself, she could feel her skin tingle with awareness of his physical closeness. And as she straightened, and turned, she felt as if her heart had stopped. It was four years since she and Derek had lived together— and during those four years she had never shared a bedroom with a man. And this man, looking down at her now with a gleam of sexual intent in his eyes, was having an effect on her that Derek had *never* had.

She cleared her throat. Wouldn't Rex Panther crow if he knew he could make the *Clarion's* Ice Woman melt without even touching her? Because he could. And she was way beyond denying it, even to herself.

But what baffled her was why was he bothering to come on so persistently to someone as ordinary as she was. Heavens, wherever he went, women must fall at his feet, toppling like ninepins at a bowling alley; and he was so gorgeous that he could have his pick of any of them: the most luscious, the most voluptuous, the most alluring, the most seductive. So why in heaven's name was he wasting time with her? Was it just because she was available, or was he perhaps one of those men who needed a steady diet of female adoration to feed his sexual self-confidence, or was it because——?

'Oh, Kate, I do love a challenge.'

There was her answer. And Rex had given it to her unknowingly as he gathered the three small bottles from her hands and placed them on the bar-top.

'Well, of course you do!' she exclaimed with deliberate airiness. 'That's why you're such a successful journalist! What could be more challenging than sitting in a pub abroad shooting the breeze with —— ?'

Laughter rolled from him with an easiness that made her draw in her breath irritably. 'You're repeating yourself, I believe. Does that mean you've run out of ammunition?'

Run out of ammunition? She couldn't even think straight while he was standing beside her, far less come up with an original insult. 'Excuse me,' she said stiffly, brushing past him, 'I'll get a couple of glasses.'

'My my, I'd never have guessed you had such a violent streak...'

Kathryn took a tumbler and a crystal wine glass from the shelf above the bar-top. If he only knew it, the thought of throwing something at him was, at this moment, very tempting indeed.

She watched without speaking as he mixed her spritzer, watched without speaking as he poured his ginger ale, but when he handed her her drink his fingers brushed lightly against her own, and the electrical spark that sizzled between them was so intense that her eyes widened in shock. And as she looked up abruptly, she saw that his tawny gaze was sparkling with fun, his lips twitching with laughter. Yet, preposterous as it seemed, the fact that he was amused at her response and making no attempt to hide his amusement did nothing to alter the fact that her legs felt as if they were going to give way at any moment.

She stumbled back, spilling a few drops of her drink as she did, and sat on the first thing she came to, which, as it happened, was the bed.

As soon as she did, she felt dismay ripple through her. What a mistake. Wouldn't Rex immediately misconstrue her reasons for choosing that particular resting-place? But she would look like a gauche teenager if she flung herself awkwardly to her feet again and went to sit somewhere else. The only thing to do was ... act like the cool and controlled woman she wanted him to think she was.

'Cheers!' Leaning back with a supreme attempt to look casual, and supporting herself with one hand on the pillows behind her, she raised her glass, and took a long sip of her spritzer.

'Good health.' Rex had moved to stand beside her, and she felt the bottom hem of the pale blue towel brush against her knees. His stomach was at the level of her eyes, and she felt mesmerised as she stared helplessly at his smooth, tanned skin, at the contrast of his crisp black hair with the icy colour of the plush towel. And all of a sudden, to her horror, she was almost overwhelmed by an insane longing to reach out and trail her fingertips across the top of the towel, to grasp the upper edges, to tug it open . . .

With one noisy gulp she drained the rest of her spritzer. She had to get him to move before she made an absolute fool of herself.

Her hand shook a little as she leaned over and placed her empty glass on the bedside table. 'Why don't you go ahead and get dressed?' she said, a slight raggedness in her tone despite her efforts to keep her voice steady. 'When you're finished in the bathroom, I'd like to have a shower before I change for dinner.'

'I'm finished in the bathroom.' He placed his empty glass beside her own. 'So you can go right ahead.' Then, with his eyes narrowed so that she couldn't see his expression, he added, 'Oh, just one thing first . . .'

'Mmm?' With an effort, Kathryn affected an expression that she hoped would pass for one of polite interest.

'While we were on the veranda with Derek——' Rex's damp hair tumbled down over his brow and he thrust his fingers through it, pushing it back '——you said there might be something I could do for you . . . later. This is later, Kate . . . and, if I recall, you also implied you were a person who didn't break her promises.'

Oh, lord, she should have known that her flippant little attempt at putting one over on him would come back to haunt her. 'I did, didn't I?' She gave a light little laugh.

'So...what's it to be, Kate?' Though his tone was playful, there was an intensity behind the words that set her heart hammering.

Frantically, she tried to come up with some answer, but even as her thoughts darted this way and that, without any success, Rex sat down on the edge of the bed, turning towards her.

'If you can't think of anything, then perhaps I can make a suggestion.'

He wasn't touching her, but he didn't need to. Despite the inches separating them, she could feel the physical pull of his body, the magnetism emanating from his naked, muscled flesh...

'A suggestion?' she echoed faintly. What did he have in mind? That she should make love with him?

'Yes,' he murmured. 'A suggestion. What I'd like to do is...take this braid——' before she could draw back, he'd reached out, and taken her braid in one hand '——and undo it.'

CHAPTER SIX

A SIGH of relief quivered through Kathryn. His request seemed harmless enough...and anyway, it would, she guessed, be useless to protest. If she did, if she tried to pull away, he would surely use the plait as a tether to keep her bound to him. So...she would let him do as he wanted; it could only take a few seconds...

'Beautiful, beautiful hair,' he murmured. Pulling off the velvet-covered band securing the end of the thick plait, he dropped it on the bedcover; and then he leaned forward, and, with his warm breath fanning her cheek, he concentrated on unwinding the three heavy ribbons of silky hair which she'd woven together that morning after she'd dressed for breakfast.

'It's a sin,' he said softly, 'to hide hair like yours. It should be loose, swinging over your shoulders, shining in all its glory for the world to see. There, that's the way I wanted it...' She felt him draw his fingers through the silky curtain, and at the same time thought she heard a quick, indrawn hiss. 'Oh, my God, Kate,' he said huskily, 'it feels even lovelier than I'd imagined. The strands slide against my skin like rays of yellow satin sunlight —— ' he buried his face in that sunlight and inhaled '—with a scent that brings memories of lazy summer afternoons and walking in alpine meadows...'

Kathryn felt her heart clench. There was such sincerity in his voice, such passion. Her body seemed to melt as she heard his words, seemed to sway towards him...

But even as it did, she recalled abruptly the words she'd spat at Rex just that morning. 'I've met men like you...men who arrogantly believe that under the trappings of every female's success is a frustrated nymphomaniac who wants nothing more than to lie back and whimper with desire and delight in the arms of any man who will have her.'

Dear God, another moment and she would find herself in just that position, if she didn't do something, say something, to defuse this tension between them.

She took his wrists and pushed his hands away, forcing herself to ignore the way her pulses leaped as her fingertips brushed his warm skin, his crisp black hair, his strong bones. 'All you asked to do was unbraid my hair,' she said breathlessly. 'You didn't say you wanted to write a poem about it.'

'I wish I could. That's not the direction where my talent lies, though...'

'You'd have liked to be a poet?' Surprise caught Kathryn short.

'No.' Rex's eyes were still fixed on her hair, which she was pulling back from her face. 'No,' he said absently, 'that's not what I want to do. I want to write a...'

He stopped abruptly.

Kathryn waited, but when he didn't go on she said, 'Go on. Write a...what?'

He seemed to hesitate, and then said quietly, 'Oh, nothing. Forget it.'

'No.' Kathryn's voice was curious. 'I don't want to forget it. Please tell me...what were you going to say? You want to write...?'

He stood up, and looked down at her. His eyes now were serious. She had never seen them more serious. 'Do you have a secret dream, Kate?'

No harm in telling him, yes, she had a secret dream—though nothing on earth would have compelled her to tell him what that dream was.

'Sure...doesn't everyone?'

'I guess. Mine, at any rate, is one that's shared by almost every journalist I've ever known.' His mouth twisted in a smile that was slightly self-derisive.

'Ah.' At last understanding, Kathryn nodded her head. 'You want to write a novel.'

'Guilty as charged, ma'am.'

Though his stance was assertive, maybe even slightly aggressive, as he spoke—his feet apart, his hands resting on his hips—to Kathryn's surprise she saw in his eyes a look of waiting, a look of vulnerability... a look that told her more clearly than any words that he was wary of what her reaction was going to be. Surely he didn't expect that she was going to laugh at him?

'I think that's wonderful!' And she did. And she found herself strangely touched that he should have confided in her. It was obvious from his manner that it wasn't a piece of information he was used to bandying about. 'Your writing is in a class by itself,' she went on. 'Have you given any thought as to the type of novel you'd like to write? Oh, that was a silly question. I'm sure you have.'

The wariness was no longer in his eyes, and she wondered if she might have imagined it. But yet she was sure she hadn't. Before she could decide, Rex spoke, and diverted her thoughts.

'I've seen so many wars, Kate,' he said, 'and so much suffering. For years I've wished I could do something to make the world a better place.' He flicked one hand in a wry gesture.

'Don't we all? Of course, it would seem like a futile goal...how can one person make a difference in the whole enormous scheme of things? But we can, and that's how it has to start...or at least that's how I see it. We can't wait for people in government to lead the way—in many cases they're so focused on achieving their own private goals, they don't want to rock the boat. But someone has to. And I'd like to write a book that would convince people they *can* change things...and how to go about it. I already have a rough outline of my plot. My two main characters—a man and a woman—are presidents of neighbouring countries, two countries which are about to go to war. What happens in the beginning of the book is these two people meet...and fall violently in love. Secretly, they become lovers...and then the woman becomes pregnant with his child...the child of the enemy. You can see the conflicts facing them, of course, and the main thrust of the book will be the struggle of the protagonists to avert war and bring their people together...for the future of their unborn child...but also, ultimately, for the future of every child...'

As he continued talking, Kathryn listened, genuinely interested, but even while she listened she also observed. Observed how changed

Rex was while he was talking about his novel. Gone was the mocking glint that was usually in his eyes when he talked to her, gone was the brash and cocky tone that so often imbued the words he spoke to her. His eyes now had a slightly far-away look, his voice had a throbbing intensity, and his body leaned towards hers in a way that, without touching, seemed to embrace her. He was opening himself up to her, in a way that he never had before. And his masculinity had never seemed more compelling, as he spoke with a force of energy and determination that melted away every last bit of hostility she felt for him.

Here was a man who was everything a man should be, she found herself thinking: not only was he devastatingly attractive and tremendously sexy, he was also a man of honour, with values in accord with her own, and with a core of decency and integrity that stole her very —

'So, Kate...'

With a great effort, she dragged her attention back to what he was saying.

'You said you had a dream, too... a secret dream. Are you going to tell me yours, now that I've told you mine?'

Her secret dream. The dream that could never come true. But even as she felt the familiar, aching pang of regret, all thoughts of her secret dream faded from her consciousness. Instead, she found herself staring at Rex, at his beautiful golden eyes, at his lean, chiselled features, at his damp tousled hair, at his sensual lips parted in a waiting smile...and as she did she felt as if the ground was opening under her and she was falling helplessly down into a great dark void.

'Oh, my God...' The words trembled from between her lips before she could stop them. She felt the colour drain from her face, felt her heartbeats stagger and threaten to stop. Unsteadily, she got to her feet.

Rex stared at her. 'Are you all right?' His voice was sharp with concern.

'I'm fine.' Kathryn's response came out in a breathy, despairing gasp.

'No, you're not! Tell me, what's the —?'

Move! Move! she ordered herself, and with a supreme effort wheeled away from him and made her stumbling way across the carpeted floor to the bathroom. 'I'm *fine*,' she repeated, her voice now so harsh that she barely recognised it, 'just a bit faint—all the heat, I suppose...or maybe the wine.' Once in the bathroom, she closed the door behind her, and, locking it, leaned against the panelling.

'Kate —'

'Would you mind,' she called, frantically dragging her loose hair back from her face, 'leaving me alone for a while? Perhaps...could you go away...could you get dressed and go downstairs...?'

There was no sound for a few moments, and then his voice, right by the door, taut but steady. 'You're sure you're all right?'

'Yes,' she answered. 'I'm sure.'

'In that case...' she sensed his reluctance '...OK, I'll leave you alone. But I'll come up for you in...about half an hour.'

'No,' she said quickly. 'Don't...come up. I'll come down.'

She stayed where she was, leaning against the door, till finally she heard him go out.

Then, and only then, did she move.

She pushed herself away and went to stand by the mirror. Staring at her reflection, she tried to see what she hadn't seen there that morning. And there they were, the tell-tale signs—the feverish flush on her cheeks, the look of dazed shock in her eyes, the tremulous quivering of her lips...

Oh, God help me, she thought, as panic swept over her like the drowning tide of a great, swelling ocean...

She had fallen in love with Rex Panther.

*   *   *

Dusk was falling when, half an hour later, she finished dressing and stepped out on to the little balcony. The air was a pot-pourri of sweet fragrances, laced with the tang of the ocean. From below came the murmur of voices, and the occasional sound of laughter.

Moving forward quietly, Kathryn curled her fingers round the top of the wrought-iron railing and glanced down to the veranda.

Flame, Derek and Rex were seated around the glass-topped table, and they were obviously enjoying a drink before dinner. Rex's, she imagined, would be non-alcoholic...

Her gaze veered straight to him and fixed on him, as if it had a mind of its own. And her heart ached agonisingly as she took in the familiar tilt of his dark head, the way the fabric of his white shirt pulled across his wide, muscled shoulders, the sound of his husky chuckle as he reacted to some amusing remark Flame had made...

After Derek had jilted her, Kathryn had never expected to fall in love again...had never wanted to fall in love again. The pain she'd felt as a result of Derek's betrayal had been unbearable; that kind of suffering was something she had had no wish to expose herself to a second time. But she *had* fallen in love again. And how ironic it was, she thought despairingly, that it was with a man who adored children. She'd sensed it already, from the disbelieving expression in his eyes when she'd told him children had no place in her plans for the future, but the mother of the little boy at the market had confirmed it for her...

'You're fond of kids. Am I right, or am I right?' she'd asked.

'Yes. As a matter of fact, I'm crazy about them,' Rex had replied, with a friendly chuckle.

'I knew it.' The woman's tone had been smug. 'That's just the kind of man you are.'

That was the kind of man he was. Kathryn sighed as she turned back into the bedroom. The kind of man who already had a home waiting for the wife and children he would eventually acquire... because that lovely bungalow in Shaugnessy was not—decidedly not—a bachelor pad. It was sitting there, invitingly, just begging for a family of its own... for a wife who would create a peaceful oasis in the busy, stressful world of today, a mother who would create a warm and cheerful place for her children to bring their friends...

It was not a house for a woman who was no longer a woman.

Kathryn realised she had walked across the room to the dresser and was staring at her reflection through eyes that were blurred with tears. But despite the tears, she could see herself ... see the glossy blonde hair hanging loose to her shoulders—the way Rex liked it, see the navy and white chiffon blouse and navy silk skirt that set off her attractive figure, see the cranberry lipstick that made her mouth look even softer, even more vulnerable.

Oh, what kind of a fool was she? What kind of vanity had made her want to encourage, to beguile, to tempt—when she had no *right* to do so?

With an anguished moan, she lifted her arms and dragged her hair savagely back from her face. A minute later, it was coiled into a prim, forbidding chignon. Then with a tissue she blotted away most of her lipstick, blindly ignoring the effect it had on her face, making it look pale and wan. There was nothing she could do about her outfit—it was the only dressy one she'd brought with her, so it would have to do—but her body language ... *that* she could do something about, and she would make sure it sent the message to Rex Panther that she was not available.

Grimly, she turned and crossed to the door, picking up her camera equipment as she went. Rex had seen something in her eyes, while he'd been sitting on the edge of the bed, that had provoked a dangerous response in him. He had seen, she was sure, the desire she had been unable to conceal in time. But he would never see it again. Cool, distant and professional—that was the relationship she wanted to have with him.

It was, she knew, the only relationship possible.

It was the only relationship that would be fair to them both.

With her lips tightly compressed, she swung her camera gear over her shoulder. Perhaps, with Flame's permission, she could shoot a roll of film while they were having dinner; perhaps then the actress would be more relaxed, and allow herself to *be* herself.

Kathryn didn't hold out much hope... but at least it gave her something else to think about, something other than her feelings for Rex.

She had, after all, come here to do a job. And from now on, that was what she was going to concentrate on.

'Tell me, Flame——' Rex threw the movie star a disarming smile as she poured him a second after-dinner cup of coffee '——a little more about your mother. You said earlier that she was a typical stay-at-home mum, the kind who was always there for you, who always made your friends feel welcome when you were growing up.'

'That's right.' Flame put the coffee-pot back on its stand in the centre of the dining-table. 'I couldn't have wished for a better mother.'

'And your father...?' Rex let his question trail casually away.

The actress had given Kathryn permission to take pictures during and after their meal; now Kathryn was sitting back from the table a little, her eye fixed on Flame through the lens of her camera. Had she not been staring at her with such intensity, had she not just focused on the perfect, heart-shaped face, she might never have noticed the almost imperceptible way the star's eyelids had flickered over the hooded green eyes...had flickered almost furtively, as she spoke.

Intrigued, she shot a couple of pictures, then, pretending to be concentrating on changing the camera speed, she scrutinised Flame's face with even more care as the star, rubbing the point of her nose—nervously, Kathryn thought— said with a bright smile,

'My father? He travelled a lot—as I told you this morning, Rex. But when he was at home, he more than made up for the long absences on the road. He called me his little cinnamon bun—cinnamon because of this, of course.'

She ran her long fingers through the mass of auburn curls rippling across her shoulders. 'I loved him dearly.'

She may have loved him dearly, Kathryn mused...but why, then, had her green eyes darkened to a deep forest-green as she spoke of him, why was that tiny vein dancing at the corner of her mouth, and why had the muscles of her neck tightened convulsively as if a cord had whipped round it, choking her?

Rex said, 'And you were an only child. Do you think your parents were disappointed that they didn't have a larger family...considering they were both so fond of children?'

Flame cleared her throat. 'Perhaps.' The star's smile seemed forced, Kathryn thought, and a second later the redhead pushed back her chair and got to her feet, as if letting them all know she wanted to put an end to the conversation. 'Shall we go outside for a while?' she asked smoothly.

'Oh, let's not,' Derek said. 'The midges are such a pest at this time of the evening.'

Kathryn snapped a picture of Flame as her slim shoulders lifted in an irritable shrug.

'Let's adjourn to the living-room, then,' the actress offered. 'Yes, that might be best. Kathryn can take some pictures of the two of us there; it really is the nicest room in the villa.

And she should get some excellent shots with the grand piano in the background, and perhaps a couple of pictures of us looking at the Picasso I bought you for Christmas.'

Despite herself, Kathryn glanced at Rex. He raised his eyebrows slightly, as if to let her know he was wondering exactly the same thing *she* was: up till now, Flame had given the impression that she wasn't interested in co-operating with Kathryn; what had caused her apparent change of attitude? It rang false, somehow.

As they all trooped across the front hall, with Flame and Derek leading the way, Rex murmured to Kathryn, 'Curiouser and curiouser.'

He had happened to brush against her as he spoke, and she felt his hair-roughened forearm graze the delicate skin of her arm. As if he'd made a pass at her, she jerked her shoulder away. She noticed his quick frown, but he said nothing.

'Sorry,' she muttered automatically. 'Static...you know... Caught me off guard.'

Certainly she had felt a jolt of electricity, but she knew full well it hadn't been static; it had been generated by his accidental touch. Had he felt it too?

'Static?' His lazy drawl was for her ears alone, as he stepped aside to let her enter the living-room before him. 'I think not, Kate. Static electricity doesn't flow as a current...and what is flowing between us is certainly electricity. And high voltage at that.' He grinned. 'Disturbing, isn't it? Like sticking your finger in a light socket!'

'I have never,' she retorted under her breath, 'been so foolish as to stick my finger in a light socket, so I haven't the faintest idea what that would feel like.'

With a wicked smile that would have given Jack Nicholson a run for his money, he brushed her arm again, and there was no mistaking it for an accident. 'This, Kate, is what it feels like.' She could feel his whisper riffling across the top of her sleekly upcoiled hair. 'Just so you'll know...next time.'

With a supreme effort, Kathryn dragged her attention from him, and settled it once more on Flame.

Tonight the actress was wearing another caftan, this one as light and gauzy as the one she'd had on in the morning; it was of pale violet chiffon, and flowed around her like a regal robe as she moved across to the rattan seating arrangement in the far corner of the room, by a wide bay window.

It was quite dark now, outside, and as Kathryn sat down on a comfortable-looking

swivel rocker she could see the lights of the
yachts in the harbour. They winked and
sparkled like a careless scattering of small dia-
monds, on the purple-navy backcloth of the
bay.

Her view was broken as Rex stepped in front
of her.

'Excuse me,' he murmured, and, walking
around the other chairs and couches, crossed
to the window. For the first time, Kathryn
noticed that the wide sill acted as a display area
for a magnificent collection of shells.

'These are wonderful,' he said. 'Were they
all gathered from local beaches?'

'Mmm.' Flame tossed back her head and her
hair shimmered like golden-auburn filament.
'Monique collects them. Dust gatherers, I call
them, but since she's the one who has to dust
them...' She shrugged, as if to say, That's her
problem.

'What a beauty this is.' About to pick up a
nine-inch tawny-shelled King Helmet conch, he
turned to Flame, his eyes seeking permission.

She waved a dismissive hand. 'Be my guest.'

'You're interested in shells?' Derek sat back
in his chair, his legs crossed at the ankles.

Rex nodded as he stroked the curve of the
shell with a careful fingertip, and smiled wryly.
'I'm a beachcomber from way back. I started

collecting shells when I was a kid—my father
and I went camping in the summers on the west
coast of Vancouver Island, and we used to find
some real treasures on the beaches there—but
it became a serious addiction only when I
started travelling the world in the course of my
work. Some of Monique's shells are rare.'

'There's a great variety of species on this
island,' Derek offered. 'Of course, that's how
it got its name—L'Ile des Coquilles...the
Island of Shells. The best beach is just south
of here—there's a curved reef offshore which
protects it.' He turned to Kathryn. 'Do you
share Rex's interest in shells, Kathryn?'

'Shells?' She realised she was rubbing the
palm of her right hand over the flat plane of
her stomach, and quickly she lifted her hand
away and folded her arms protectively across
her chest. 'I've...never paid much attention
to them... I certainly don't know very much
about them.' She shrugged. 'They're pretty
enough, I suppose...but they're...empty.'

'Empty?' Rex was holding the shell to his ear
as he spoke. He was looking at her, but his eyes
were slightly unfocused, as if he wasn't really
listening to her, but to something else. 'Strange,
I never think of them as empty.'

Kathryn got to her feet. This was one line of
conversation she had no interest in pursuing.

'You were saying, Flame, you'd like me to take some pictures in here?'

Flame glanced up at her indifferently. 'If you wish.'

My heavens, Flame, what enthusiasm! 'Derek, would you sit with Flame on the couch there? Good, that's fine.' Kathryn raised her gaze to Rex, who was still standing with the conch to his ear. 'You'll have to move, Rex,' she said coolly. 'Unless you want to be in these shots too.'

He put down the shell, and moved out of the way, coming to stand beside her. 'Sorry,' he said. 'Perhaps I can ask Flame some more questions while you're working. Your parents, Flame—how much of an influence over your choice of career do—?'

'No.' Flame waved a dismissing hand through the air. 'No more questions tonight. Let's do one thing at a time. Tomorrow, Rex, I promise you, we'll have another session together before you leave.' She drew back her lips and threw Kathryn a travesty of a smile. 'Go ahead, Kathryn. Derek and I are all yours.'

CHAPTER SEVEN

ALL yours, indeed!

As Kathryn closed her camera two hours later, she felt even angrier than she'd felt after her photographic session in the afternoon. Though Derek had co-operated to the full, Flame had once again deliberately ruined every chance for a successful series of shots.

An hour or so into the session, Flame had decided she didn't need Derek any longer, and the latter had invited Rex to play a game of billiards. They had gone out of the room together, and hadn't come back. But now, as Flame saw Kathryn close her camera, she said in a peremptory tone, 'Just a few more, then we'll wrap it up for the night.'

Kathryn bit back a retort and with a taut smile she opened the camera again. But after she'd shot only two or three pictures Flame said rudely, 'Oh, for God's sake put that thing away.'

Kathryn's anger, which had been simmering all evening, suddenly erupted to a full boil.

144

She rammed her camera into its case and hooked the strap over her shoulder. 'Fine. But before I go upstairs, there's something I'd like to say to you. I resent the fact that you've brought me all the way to the Caribbean just to make a *fool* of me. I resent the fact that you have gone out of your way to be as uncooperative as you possibly can. What I don't know...and can't even begin to imagine, is what possible satisfaction you can hope to get by having me fail so miserably in this assignment—because fail I certainly shall! No editor in his right mind would want to buy the pictures I've been taking here. Are you doing this just because I was once engaged to Derek? Because you want, in some perverted way, to get back at me? Good grief, what kind of a mind do you have, to come up with such a twisted scenario? I'll tell you something, Ms Cantrell—as an actress you may be tops, but, as a person, in my book you rate less than a lousy zero!'

Oh, lord, she'd really blown it now. She could just imagine Ken's purple face exploding as he listened to Flame's furious report on the phone—a report she would certainly give as soon as she possibly could. Kathryn closed her eyes briefly. Cool, distant, professional. Wasn't that how she'd decided earlier she wanted to present herself, for the remainder of her stay on the island? Well, that was a laugh. Her behaviour would have made a fishwife look like a graduate from a finishing school...

'It's a bad workman who blames his tools...or in your case, Miss Ashby, a poor photographer who blames her subject.' Flame's voice, chillingly cold, filled the silence in the room. 'From the way Derek has always sung your praises, I had expected more of you...much, much more.'

'Derek has nothing to do with this,' Kathryn retorted. But even as the challenging words echoed in her ears, she wondered about the truth of them. Rex had already surmised that she herself was somehow involved in whatever was going on here...

'Don't you think —— ' Kathryn tried as hard as she could to keep her voice steady, to keep her anger from spilling over any further '——it's time you put your cards on the table and tell me why you *really* brought me to the island?'

Flame inhaled deeply, her nostrils quivering. 'I brought you here for one reason only. I *detest* dealing with the media, and I decided that if I were to break my rule of not talking to the Press and not permitting journalists or photographers into my home, then perhaps there wouldn't be the same incentive for the pa-

parazzi to keep hounding me. And naturally, for this session, which I intend to be a one-off, I wanted a top-calibre photographer——'

'Hogwash!' The word came spitting from Kathryn. 'The only person you're fooling with that story is yourself. It certainly doesn't fool me.' She bit her lip and stared at the actress, wondering if she dared go on or not. And then she decided recklessly, what the heck? As well be hung for a sheep as a lamb.

She took in a deep breath. 'Whatever the real reason——' she managed to keep her voice level '——I hope you think it was worth the effort. Personally, I believe that you've been wasting your time. We'll be leaving tomorrow, and, as far as I can see, all your ingenious plotting has achieved nothing... other than setting Derek off on a drinking binge!' Oh, lord, she had really torn it now. But she didn't care. Her photographic assignment had been shot to hell anyway; she had nothing to lose. Turning away from the actress, she started striding towards the door and had almost reached it when she heard Flame's voice calling after her.

'Stop!'

Kathryn froze with her hand curved around the door-handle. What did the woman want now—and how dared she call after her so haughtily? But though Kathryn heard an urgent inner voice telling her to ignore the movie star's harsh command, she also heard another voice, a more insidious one, whispering that perhaps she should obey. Granted, Flame's tone had been loud and imperious . . . yet surely it had held an edge of . . . something that had sounded almost like panic.

Panic? Why would Flame be starting to panic? Curiosity suddenly got the better of Kathryn, and, making an impulsive decision, she uncurled her fingers from the door-handle, and turned round.

'What do you want?' she asked.

'I want you to come back.' Flame's gesture was abrupt.

Treading slowly, Kathryn walked back to the centre of the room, where she hesitated.

'Sit down.' The star was toying impatiently with a huge emerald pendant hanging in the V-neck of her caftan.

Kathryn perched on the arm of a sturdy chair and watched with wary eyes as Flame began to pace restlessly around the room. After what seemed to Kathryn an endless wait, the redhead stopped pacing, and turned to her. Her eyes seemed more hooded than ever, her expression shuttered.

'You and Derek were once engaged. Apparently you had even got to the point where

you were making arrangements for the
wedding.' Her voice was taut. 'What I brought
you here for was ... I want to know what happened between you to cause you to break up.'

Kathryn stared at her blankly. The other
woman had gone to these great lengths, these
convoluted lengths, simply to find out why
Derek had jilted her? 'He hasn't told you?' Her
voice was incredulous.

'No.' Flame gave the pendant a frustrated
little tug. 'He hasn't. And,' she added with a
flare of temper, 'I don't think that a man who
plans to marry should have secrets from his
future wife. So if *he* won't tell me, then I have
no option but to get the information from you.'

But that information was something Kathryn
was not prepared to give. She suddenly felt very
weary, and her tone revealed that weariness as
she said, 'I'm sorry. It's not something I want
to discuss.'

'I can't think why it has to be such a secret!'
The redhead's voice had a ragged edge. 'Derek
told me he was the one who broke it off, but
if that's true then why ... ?'

She broke off suddenly.

'Why ... what?' Kathryn felt her pulse
quicken. At last, she thought, they were getting
close to the root of the problem ... whatever
that problem was.

Flame whirled away from her and crossed to the French doors, where silk curtains fluttered in the breeze from the ocean. Kathryn thought she heard a shuddering sigh.

'Why...what?' she persisted, a *frisson* of anticipation skimming down her spine as she got up from the arm of the chair. 'What were you going to say?'

She was beginning to think Flame hadn't heard her, when the other woman at last turned round again, very slowly.

'If Derek was the one who broke it off ——' her arms were held rigidly at her sides '——then why does he always have such a look of unhappiness in his eyes whenever your name comes up? Why won't he talk about it? I think ——' it seemed to take a great effort for her to go on '——I think he's lied to me. I think...*he* wasn't the one to break it off. I think it was...you.'

'You're wrong, it ——'

'I've suspected it for some time.' Flame's shrill accusing words trembled right over the top of Kathryn's. 'And then, today, when Rex said you'd gone straight to his bed from Derek's, I knew I'd been right. You weren't jilted, were you? It was *you* who jilted *Derek*.'

The actress's face had become ashen...so much so that Kathryn felt a twinge of concern, despite the way the other woman had treated her. 'No,' she said, 'you've got it all wrong. Derek *was* the one who broke off our engagement. But why on earth does it matter to you who did the jilting?' Kathryn couldn't hide her confusion. 'Surely all that matters now is that you love Derek, and he loves you ——'

'*But does he*?' Almost before the words were out of her mouth, Flame's hands flew up to her lips to cover them, but it was too late. And as Kathryn stared, disbelievingly, she saw the hooded green eyes become bright. With *tears*? Yes, Kathryn realised, the glinting was caused by tears. As she stared disbelievingly at the movie star, she saw her perfect features twist into a mask of despair. And with a little mewing sound in her throat, Flame sank down on to the nearest armchair and put her head in her hands.

Good lord...

Kathryn stood still for a long moment, unsure what to do, or what to say. The possibility slipped into her head that Flame was putting on a huge act for some reason...but as soon as the idea took shape Kathryn dismissed it. The sobs now coming from the depths of the armchair were too heart-rending to be anything but genuine.

'I saw you,' Flame choked out, as, raising her head and pushing her hair back from her face, she looked up at Kathryn. Kathryn saw that her eyes were now swimming with tears. 'I saw the two of you holding hands today, I saw Derek kissing you . . . and when I've asked him about you in the past —— ' the redhead's voice was threaded with misery '——he's always been evasive. Why would he be that way, if . . . if he didn't still . . . want you?'

And with the sudden explosive clarity of a mega-watt light bulb flashing on in her head, Kathryn at last realised why Flame had been treating her with so much hostility. The actress mistakenly believed that Derek was still in love with her.

If the situation weren't so sad, it would be laughable; Flame, one of the world's most beautiful women, jealous of someone like herself, someone who could walk down the street without attracting a second glance.

Kathryn shook her head, a wry smile on her lips. 'You're way off base—in fact, you couldn't be more wrong. What you saw this morning was just . . . two people making a tentative step back towards friendship. Derek's in love with *you* . . . He told me so this morning. He told me you were the only woman in the world for him. As to why he hasn't told you

why he broke off with me, I'm afraid you'll
have to ask him about that. He may not tell
you, though, and if you love him I advise you
to take him on trust. It has nothing to do with
you, or your relationship with him.'

'You're...not...still in love with him, then?
You really are...in love with...Rex?'

Flame rubbed her knuckles over her eyes,
smearing her mascara over her cheekbones, and
in a very distant part of Kathryn's mind she
couldn't help thinking that if she could just
photograph the star now, her picture might
even hit the front cover of *Time*.

'No.' She shook her head firmly. 'I fell out
of love with him when he broke off our engagement. And as for my relationship with
Rex—that's a private matter.'

It had been a crazy evening...but what
Kathryn found so hard to understand was why
Flame had broken down, emotionally, in front
of her...revealing so much of herself. The actress surely had to be a very strong person to
have survived in the movie world the way she
had, which made it all the more baffling that
she had fallen to pieces in front of a complete
stranger. It didn't seem to be consistent with
the woman's character. It just didn't fit...

'I'm...ashamed of myself.' Flame stood up,
wobbling a little. 'Ashamed of the way I've

been with you. You seem like a . . . nice person. You probably are a nice person. From a nice family.' Her face threatened to crumple again as she mentioned family. 'I lied to you . . . and I lied to Rex,' she whispered. 'Everything . . . about my own family . . . it was all lies. My life —— ' she gave a hysterical little laugh '—it's all been one big lie.'

Kathryn tried to battle the confusion in her head; too much was happening. Too much, all at once, for her to take it all in. 'What on earth are you talking about?'

'My father . . . he didn't want children. When he found out my mother was expecting me . . . he walked out on her.' Her laughter had stopped abruptly. 'I knew nothing about him. My mother hated him so much she never ever talked about him.'

'But . . . he called you his cinnamon bun . . .'

'I made that up. I made everything up. I didn't want to admit to myself that my own father had walked out on me.'

Kathryn fumbled in her mind for something to say, but before she could come up with anything remotely adequate Flame went on,

'That's why I've always felt so . . . insecure . . . with Derek. I've always tried to be perfect for him, so he wouldn't leave me.' She brushed a tear from her cheek. 'I've always been so afraid that something about me would make him walk away...if anything changed. And now—especially now...'

'Especially...now?'

Flame moaned. 'I'm afraid to tell Derek. Oh, dear God...what will I do if he leaves me? How can I tell him...?'

'Tell him what?' But even as Kathryn asked the question, she felt a leaden sinking feeling in the pit of her stomach. She knew what Flame was going to say before she opened her mouth to say it...to say the words she herself at one time would have given the world to say. Flame didn't need to say the words, but she couldn't have known that Kathryn had guessed them already.

'I'm expecting Derek's baby,' the star whispered.

It was well after midnight when Kathryn finally stole upstairs.

When she reached her bedroom, she made sure she made no noise as she opened the door. The room was in darkness, and there was no way of telling whether or not Rex was in bed; if he was, she had no wish to disturb him. The only light was the moonlight filtering in through the shutters, and through the half-open door to the balcony.

Carefully laying her camera equipment on a cushioned chair, she began tiptoeing her way to the bathroom.

She was almost there when she heard Rex's voice.

'Hi, there...'

Grimacing, she was about to reply, when he went on, 'Yes, I thought you'd just be finishing dinner—the four-hour time difference...'

He must be talking on the phone, and his voice seemed to be coming from outside. Peering in the direction of the balcony, Kathryn saw a vague outline—Rex's outline—just beyond the French doors; he was standing out in the moonlight, the phone at his ear. His back was to her; apparently he hadn't heard her come in.

'Dinner on Monday night?' he was saying. 'Your place or mine? Great, I'll look forward to it.' He chuckled. 'I can't wait to see the lady in my life again...'

The lady in his life.

'OK, Laura,' he went on softly, 'I'll call you when I get back.'

He had told her he didn't have a wife...but he had never said he didn't have a lady in his life. If she'd known he had one, would it have made this weekend easier? Would it have helped her to cope with his teasing, his flirting? For teasing and flirting were all that it amounted to. She hadn't realised just how much more she had been reading into it ...

He was talking again, in a tone of warm affection. But even as the words came floating to her, Kathryn pressed her hands to her ears.

Eavesdropping; that was what she was doing. Her cheeks flushed as embarrassment flooded through her. Whirling around, she hurried silently back to the door, and, opening it without a sound, slipped out into the hall again. Taking a deep breath, she opened it a second time, and, making no effort to be quiet, flicked on the light and walked into the room.

She saw Rex turn. He acknowledged her with a nod, and then turned sideways, presenting his profile to her as he continued with his conversation. His voice was lower now, his words inaudible.

Kathryn walked across to the stand where Rex had laid her weekend bag, and began rummaging in it for her pink cotton nightgown ... and, as she did, wasn't surprised to see that her hands were trembling. It had been quite a day ... and quite an evening.

And she didn't want to think of all the things that had happened. All she wanted to do was get washed and changed and into bed before

Rex finished on the phone. And then she would will herself to go to sleep.

She would close her mind to thoughts of Flame and Derek, close it to the long talk she and Flame had had after Flame's quavering announcement, the long talk during which she, Kathryn, had—without revealing why Derek had broken their engagement—convinced Flame that Derek would welcome with a joyous heart the news that he was to become a father.

Of course, she knew now why Flame had seemed so overly emotional; it was a well-known fact that pregnant women were prone to see-sawing mood swings. And this side-effect of pregnancy had obviously been responsible for intensifying the jealousy she was harbouring towards Kathryn herself, causing her to become so obsessed with the past—the past shared by Derek and Kathryn—that she had behaved in a manner that was far from rational.

So Kathryn decided to close her mind to it . . . as she knew she would also have to close her mind to her discovery that she was in love with Rex. Even if she hadn't been going to do that anyway, because any relationship between them would have been, for her, a dead end of the heart, now that she knew there was already someone in his life she had no choice.

Without letting her eyes stray again to the balcony, she made for the bathroom. But when, a few minutes later, while she was brushing her hair, she heard Rex whistling in the bedroom, the promises she'd made to herself scattered like dry leaves in a winter gale. Just the sound of his whistling was enough to draw a yearning from her heart. She'd never been in love before—she realised that now—so how could she have been expected to know that falling in love could make her feel so reckless, so out of control? How could she have been expected to know that it would create such a desperate wanting in her —— ?

'You can't linger in there much longer, Katie, my love.' She could tell that he was standing right by the door; she could almost feel his body heat reaching out to her. 'Come on out—unless you've something to hide. Oh, lord, you're not one of those monstrous creatures who turn into a werewolf at midnight, are you?'

She didn't look in the mirror; she didn't need to. She knew only too well how she looked. Her hair was loose—she never could sleep with it tied back—and it fell with silky seductiveness to her shoulders. Her cheeks were flushed, her eyes glittering as if she had a fever, her lips pink and full and begging to be kissed. Her nightie was cool and short, barely covering her thighs ... but when she'd packed, she had not, of course, expected to be sharing a bedroom ...

The door-handle rattled.

She grasped it firmly, as if it were a nettle, and pulled the door open.

'All right!' The tension twanging inside her made her voice taut. 'I'm coming.'

Without looking at him, she made to walk past him. But he stopped her, his hand firmly grasping her arm. Her breath caught in her throat ...

'How did it go, Kate?'

He just wanted to talk about her session with Flame. Well, what had she thought he might want to talk about? They were, after all, just business colleagues. Just friends. Suddenly, all the sparkle his touch had set bubbling in her veins just fizzed out and died.

'Everything's all right.' Her tone was flat. Perhaps even stand-offish. But as she saw the weariness in his eyes, the tired lines bracketing his mouth, she felt a rush of concern. He looked absolutely exhausted. And not only that; of course, he must be just as worried as she'd been that their trip here was going to turn out to be a waste of time. At least she could put his mind at rest about that.

'Flame opened up to me,' she said quietly. 'Tomorrow, she's going to tell you things she's never told anyone before. And she's promised me the pictures of a lifetime.' His hand was still on her bare arm, detaining her, and she felt as if it were burning her skin. As casually as she could, she drew it from his grasp. 'I'm off to bed now. It's late.'

He didn't try to stop her, but as she crossed to the bed she heard him murmur, 'Good girl.' Then as she brushed aside the mosquito netting, and slipped under the thin cotton sheet, she heard the bathroom door click shut behind him.

With a sigh, she slid across the mattress to the far side of the bed. There, she turned, so that her back would be to him. The mattress, she'd calculated, was at least seven feet wide, ample room for them both to spread out without touching each other.

But even knowing that, she curled up into a ball, so close to the edge that if she moved even two or three inches she knew she'd be in danger of falling on to the floor.

With her breath caught in her throat, her eyes squeezed tightly shut, and her heartbeats hammering out of control, she waited for him to come out of the bathroom and join her.

CHAPTER EIGHT

'GOOD morning, Kate!' Rex's cheerful greeting was accompanied by a gentle slap on Kathryn's rump.

Drowsily, she blinked, and then forced her heavy eyelids open.

Rex was up... and if his alert expression was anything to go by he'd been up for a while. The bedroom light was on, the mosquito net had been thrown aside, and he was standing by the bed, a grin on his lean face...

And nothing on his lean body but a pair of brief black swimming-trunks.

Kathryn dropped her eyelids again quickly. In a crystal-clear flash of memory, she recalled the night they had spent together. He had come to bed a few minutes after she herself had slid between the sheets, but to her astonishment— to her *disappointment*?—he hadn't even touched her. After a long yawn and a mumbled 'Goodnight, Kate' he'd adjusted the pillows under his head without waiting for a response—she'd heard the rustle of fabric, the punching sound as he moulded the pillows to the desired shape—and within seconds, it seemed, his breathing had become deep and regular, signalling that he'd drifted off to sleep. While she, burning as if she had a tropical fever, had tossed and turned half the night, wanting she knew not what—or, if she knew it, she wouldn't admit it, even to herself.

'We can't go back to Vancouver without having had a dip in the pool,' he teased her now, and as she groaned and made to bury her face in the pillow she felt his hands grasping her by the shoulders.

'Uh-uh!' He pulled her up to a sitting position. 'I know you're still sleepy—it's the time difference, of course. It's six o'clock here, though back home it's only two...'

Kathryn groaned again as he dragged her off the bed, and set her up straight as if he were arranging a toy soldier. 'I don't want to swim, darn you!' she complained, and tugged the strap of her nightie up over her shoulder as she realised it had slipped partway down her upper arm. 'I just want another hour of sleep. For heaven's sake, it's still pitch-dark outside——'

'Here, put this on.'

She stared blearily at the primrose-yellow bikini he was dangling in front of her. 'Where did you get that?' she demanded, all of a sudden wide awake and bristling like an enraged hedgehog. 'Who gave you the right to rummage in my bag——?'

'We've just shared a bed.' His voice was throaty and filled with amusement. 'I think that that more than gives me the right. Don't you agree?'

'We didn't share the bed.' She realised the words were fairly spitting from her mouth. 'We just happened to...be sleeping on the same mattress!'

Rex's chuckle had a mocking edge. 'Pity the man who marries you, Kate Ashby... Your temper is even worse first thing in the morning than it is during the day.'

'I am not *going* to get married!' She snatched her bikini from his hand as she glared up at him. 'And if I were, it would certainly never be to someone as...as *arrogant* and bossy as you!'

Laughter twinkled in his eyes. 'Is that all the thanks I get? Surely I deserve a little more——'

'Thanks?' Kathryn twisted her features into an expression of incredulity. 'Thanks for what? For wakening me at this ungodly hour?'

'For leaving your virtue intact last night.' His eyes had the opulent glint of old gold as they ran over her in a warm caress. 'It wasn't easy, I can tell you...'

'Oh, it wasn't that difficult, either,' she returned heatedly. 'You were snoring almost before your head hit the...'

She broke off with an abrupt exclamation as she saw Rex's mouth twitch. 'Yes, Katie? Go on—I was snoring almost before my head hit the pillow? Actually, I was out for the count... All my travelling seemed to catch up on me...'

As he spoke, Kathryn found herself remembering what Trish had said about Rex being burned-out. Exhausted as he was, then, it should have been no surprise to her that he'd flaked right out. The knowledge should have made her feel better...but somehow, it didn't...

'But did I detect a trace of anger there?' he was now saying in a teasing tone. 'Maybe even...disappointment?'

'You're crazy.' Kathryn hoped he hadn't noticed the way the blood had flooded to her cheeks. 'As far as I'm concerned, you're nothing but a business colleague. I have no feelings for you whatsoever... At least,' she amended with a sarcastic curl of her lip, 'no *positive* feelings.'

'Then why are you afraid to swim with me?'

'I'm not afraid to swim with you.' Her body felt as if it was streaming with perspiration, even though the morning was still cool and there was a trace of damp in the air. She had heard rain fall during the night. It was *still* night, for heaven's sake!

'Then come on. I won't touch you —— ' he raised his right hand in the Boy Scout salute '—on my honour as a scout.'

He was irresistible. Irritating, yes...and sometimes even downright obnoxious. But yet...when he set out to charm, as he was doing now...he was irresistible.

'All right.' Was that really her voice? Good lord, did she have no defences against this man? Did he just have to whistle and she came running? It seemed that way...but, of course, he didn't have to know it. And wouldn't he be more likely to believe she was indifferent to him if she didn't make such a fuss about swimming with him? She lifted her shoulders in a deliberately careless shrug. 'Just give me a minute to get changed.'

'I'll see you down there, and —— ' he touched a finger to her lips '—don't make a noise... The rest of the household's asleep. We want to have the pool to ourselves.'

He was swimming lengths when she emerged from the house and slipped like a shadow to the pool area.

She couldn't see very much at first, but as her eyes grew accustomed to the dim light she could see the top of his head as he moved smoothly through the water. With quiet, powerful strokes he cut his way from one end to the other, and despite the invisible armour Kathryn had erected around herself and her emotions as she had changed into her bikini she still felt a trace of resentment as she watched him. She certainly didn't consider herself beautiful ... yet she knew she wasn't totally unattractive either! So why—tired or not—had Rex Panther not even *attempted* to make a pass at her last night before he fell asleep? It didn't do much for her self-confidence, that was for sure.

She dropped her towel by the poolside and quickly dived into the water, unwilling to give him an opportunity to see even the outline of her bikini-clad figure. When she surfaced, she pushed her hair from her face, and trod water, looking up at the sky.

Dawn would break soon; there was just the faintest streak of lemon-pink far away, on the horizon. With a lazy sigh, she slid on to her back, weaving her hands gently to keep herself afloat.

'Glad you came, huh?'

She turned her head, to find Rex right beside her. His black hair was plastered to his skull, his teeth gleaming white as he smiled.

The water was warm, she felt totally relaxed, and she found herself smiling back at him. 'Yes,' she said, 'I'm glad I came. It's beautiful out here.'

By the ethereal glow of the underwater lighting, Kathryn saw water trickling down his face. One drop slid over his cheek, to settle in the corner of his mouth. Kathryn found herself transfixed by the sight. She felt her breathing quicken, felt her eyelids flicker. His lips were slightly parted, and they glistened...invitingly.

She realised that she had never in her life wanted anything more than to be kissed by this man; and she realised too that her feet had drifted down. She was now treading water—as was Rex. And they were so close that when she fluttered her hands under the surface they brushed against his thigh.

She felt as if every cell in her body had sprung to attention, every muscle had tautened, every nerve had become sensitised.

'I'm sorry,' she whispered, but, try as she might, she couldn't drag her gaze from his mouth.

'I'm not.' His breath was warm on her cheek. 'Kiss me, Kate...'

A lump had formed in her throat. 'You ... promised you wouldn't touch me.' Her words stumbled, as uncertain of where they were going as she was of herself.

'But *you* made no promises, Kate.'

He was right. She had made no promises. What harm would there be in kissing him? None, every voice inside her clamoured. None, none, none ...

Was this how Ulysses had felt when, bound to the mast, he heard the song of the Sirens, with its seductive magic? Had he felt spellbound, enchanted, as she was feeling now? Had all his will drained away, had there been nothing left but a wanting so desperate that he might have thought the world well lost for the heart's desire they promised him?

It took only a faint flutter of her hands in the water to move her body close enough so that she could lift her face to his. Time seemed to crack, and wait, as for a breathless moment she stared up into his eyes, feeling as if she were suspended in space ... as if they were suspended in space together, over a bottomless, dangerous chasm. And then the sheer intensity of the physical attraction pulsing between them made their coming together a thing no longer in Kathryn's control, drawn to the man beside her by forces so primal that nothing existed but this craving, this hunger, to touch her flesh to his. Her sigh was ragged as she glided her hands around his waist for support, and surrendered to the compelling need that was building inside her like a dangerous storm.

His lips were cool as she brushed hers against them tentatively, searchingly... but it seemed that his control was as frail as her own. With a swiftness that drew her breath away, he took charge and the kiss became a lover's kiss, intimate, demanding, erotic.

Their mouths clung together, greedily, hungrily, his lips no longer cool, but warm, hers no longer tentative, but eager. Sensual and persuasive, his flesh moved so skilfully on hers that it drove shafts of desire like great silver lances deep inside her. The kiss gradually became even more penetrating, Rex's tongue sliding between her parted lips, making her blood pulse thickly so that she felt a throbbing heaviness in her veins. Vaguely, she became aware that Rex had one arm around her, and with the other he was pulling her towards the side of the pool... where the wide, frondy leaves of the coconut palms would add to the shield provided by the darkness, should anyone be watching from the upper windows of the villa.

She could hear the sound of birdsong in the air, sweet and harmonious, as the small creatures began to stir; she could smell a faint heavenly fragrance wafting from the flowers around the pool, as the blossoms readied themselves for the awakening kiss of the sun...

She could feel Rex's hair-roughened thighs scraping against the smooth curve of her own thighs as she drifted into the waiting embrace of his body. Their legs became a tangle, a tangle from which she had no wish to escape. Under the water, his hand brushed against her breast, her nipple darting to life as it responded to the searching touch of his fingertips. Pleasure, an exquisite torture, quicksilvered its way to every throbbing erotic zone in her body; blind need had long since silenced all the warning signals usually sent out by the saner part of her mind. With a low moan, she slipped her fingers down the lower part of his spine, and then inside the waistband of his trunks, spreading her palms over his tautly muscled buttocks.

'Oh, God, Kate...' Rex's protest was an anguished groan, a groan that only served to intensify the ache that had begun to swell the hidden nub of her desire, swelling it till she felt it burning like an insatiable fire.

Nothing existed but this moment, this wild, pulsating moment...

His lips were at her throat; she arched her head back, far back, her breasts rising from the water. She felt his fingers dragging down the bikini top, felt the heated flesh of his lips surround the eager satin bead of her wet nipple, felt him caress the hard, dusky pearl with his tongue till the pleasure became a dazzling torture.

Dazedly, she became aware that he in turn had slipped a hand around her back, pushing down the scrap of cotton that was her bikini bottom, cupping and kneading her firm flesh; mindlessly she yielded as he pulled her lower body against his groin, feeling excitement thrill dizzily through her as she realised just how aroused he was. His trunks were of a thin fabric... as was her bikini bottom. It was as if there was nothing at all between them; they might as well have been naked.

Insistently, and in a way older than time itself, he made his needs known. And with his cheek pressed to hers, his lips against her ears, he whispered words of enticement, carnally inviting words, in a husky voice—words that made her blood run hot, and drew a moan from her throat. With his fingertips, he tantalised her, weakening her further, teasing the peak of her breast, rubbing the hard crest with its satin-soft skin, rolling it, with movements so exquisitely tender that she thought she would die with the bliss of it. So enraptured was she that she had barely noticed that he was insistently, coaxingly, trying to nudge his thigh between her legs...and when she did, her heart stopped for a second...

And she resisted...

For a second.

Yielding, she felt his pressure against her most sensitive flesh, making it swollen and enflamed, till it felt like a wild, concentrated fire. The heat of it, the intensity of it...and the aching ecstasy of it...was almost more than she could bear.

Involuntarily, she gave a little cry. It sounded, she thought in a distant part of her mind, like a plea for help.

'I want you, darling Kate.' Rex's voice, low and almost unrecognisable, was as sweet and thick as rich honey. His teeth nipped the shell-pink flesh of her earlobe with a desperate urgency. 'God help me.' He sounded like a man in pain. 'I want you.'

I want you too. She wanted to say the words, but she couldn't. She no longer had any control of herself...and she no longer felt the water that lapped around her, no longer heard the sound of birdsong, no longer smelled the fragrance of the flowers. All she was conscious of was the desire that was washing over her and over her like endless, inexorable waves...

And the burning ache that was becoming more torturous by the moment, the ache that could not be denied.

The ache that had to be fulfilled.

She could tell by Rex's voice that he was consumed by the same urgency, consumed by the same wild, frenzied need, as his muscled arm tightened in a convulsive movement around her. 'The beach, Kate,' he whispered tautly. 'We'll go down to the beach—we'll have all the privacy there that——'

The gigantic splash in the water behind them made them both jump.

'What the——?' Rex bit off his startled, frustrated exclamation as Derek's voice burst into the still air.

''Morning, love birds!' he shouted cheerily, as he splashed his way across the pool towards them. 'Saw you coming out...and decided to join you. Flame's coming down too. She's decided to have Kathryn take some pictures of us in the pool.'

Thank heavens it was still dark! With frantic fingers Kathryn fumbled for the cups of her bikini and quickly tugged them into position again. She didn't look at Rex...but she knew exactly how he must be feeling; she could hear his harsh, uneven breathing. Her frustration, she could tell, was matched only by his own.

But she had to admire his acting ability. His greeting as Derek grasped the rail beside him was a masterpiece of nonchalance.

'Well, hi to you too. It's a wonderful morning for a swim...but Kathryn here has a little problem with the strap of her bikini, and I've been trying to fix it—not making a very good job of it, though!'

'That's right.' Kathryn made an effort to sound casual too. 'I'm going to go in now, anyway, and have a shower. Tell Flame I'll be down in about ten minutes.'

Without waiting for a response from Derek, she swam quickly across to the nearest ladder, and hauled herself from the water. Picking up her towel, she draped it around herself, and as she made for the stair leading up to the bedrooms called over her shoulder, 'See you when I come back, Rex. Enjoy your swim.'

The warning in her tone had been veiled, but she knew he would get the message. She didn't want him to follow her to the bedroom. What had happened there in the water had been a mistake...a huge mistake. But thank heavens Derek had arrived and prevented what would have been a mistake of such gigantic proportions that Kathryn could barely believe she'd been about to make it.

To go down to the beach and make love with Rex Panther.

A man who already had 'a lady in his life'.

She shivered . . . and the shiver wasn't caused by the cool morning air.

It was caused by the realisation that she had been within a hair's breadth of becoming prey to the *Clarion's* own pet Panther.

'I told Flame everything,' Derek said in a quiet voice.

It was midday, and he and Kathryn were on the veranda. She was standing by the low wall, watching Rex and Flame as they strolled together along the beach below; Derek was sitting on one of the deck-chairs beside her.

'It might have been better —— ' she glanced down at him, her expression sympathetic '—if you had told her a long time ago.'

'You're right.' There was deep shame in Derek's tone. 'But I was afraid if I did she would think badly of me.'

Neither spoke for several long moments. Then Kathryn, after a brief hesitation, ventured to say, 'I was shocked to discover Flame is so . . . insecure.'

'Incredible, isn't it?' Derek scraped a hand through his dark hair. 'But she isn't the first beautiful woman to suffer from low self-esteem.'

'No,' Kathryn murmured. 'That's true.'

'Flame's possessiveness, her jealousy, have been a problem from day one of our relationship. Now that she's finally managed to open up about her background... which goes a long way to explaining why she is the way she is... I hope that'll be the first step to a more positive outlook.' He sighed. 'And to think what brought all this to a head was your winning your award.'

'My award?'

'Mmm. I was happy for you when I read about it in the newspaper. Thrilled, actually.' He frowned. 'But Flame read something into my interest that wasn't there, and before I knew it she'd become obsessed. Obsessed with you and obsessed with our past relationship... and obsessed with the idea of *seeing* you. I thought I'd managed to convince her I loved only her; I told her time and time again that she'd nothing to worry about, that I was no longer in love with you...'

Kathryn made a self-deprecatory gesture as she commented, 'She must have been stunned to discover I was such an ordinary-looking ——'

'Kathryn Ashby——' Derek lurched to his feet '——there's nothing remotely ordinary about you. You're one of the most beautiful women I've ever known. It's no wonder,' he added, 'that Panther's in love with you. Lord, I've never *seen* a man so besotted.'

'Derek...' Kathryn hesitated.

'What is it?'

'Flame knows...that what you told her about me is...not common knowledge?'

Derek nodded. 'Your secret's safe with her, Kathryn. She'll never breathe a word. She won't even mention it to Rex...unless, of course, he brings the matter up...'

Which he would never do, Kathryn reflected dully, since he would never know. 'Good,' she said in a light voice, then deliberately she turned her attention again to the couple on the beach. 'Oh,' she said, 'they're on their way back now. Shall we go down the steps and meet them?'

'Yes,' Derek agreed. 'Let's do that.'

Flame and Rex, if appearances were anything to go by, had enjoyed their long walk together...and Kathryn had no doubt that Rex's private session with the star had been as satisfactory and productive as Kathryn's own photographic session at the pool had been...

Dawn had been breaking as she'd returned downstairs with her camera, the rising sun creating a backdrop to her pictures that had almost taken her breath away. And Flame had been in an exuberant mood. Kathryn had taken some fantastic shots... several of which she knew would be winners. *Weekends Wonderful* would indeed have a memorable spread on the Saturday the Flame Cantrell issue was made available to the public.

Now, with Derek at her side, she began walking down the steps that led to the beach. But as the other couple came towards them, and she noted the arrogant swing of Rex's walk, the dark attractiveness of his lean features, she found her thoughts returning to what Derek had said.

'I've never seen a man so besotted.'

It was not, of course, true. Lust-driven, perhaps, or even momentarily diverted by her, because of her proximity. But he already had a 'lady in his life', a lady called Laura. And because of this, when Rex threw her a warm, private, intimate smile as they all met down on the beach, she pretended she didn't see it. Instead, she turned her attention to Flame, who today was wearing a gauzy cream sundress.

'I think,' Kathryn said, 'I'll go upstairs and pack my things. The helicopter will be here soon to pick us up.'

'Oh, you've got loads of time.' Flame tossed back her head and her hair glistened like copper beech leaves in a shower of autumn rain. 'Rex wants to take a walk round the headland to the beach we were talking about last night . . . and you must go with him. No one should ever visit L'Ile des Coquilles without seeing the Bay of Shells.' She took Derek's arm and looked up adoringly at him. 'And I want to spend some time alone with this man of mine. We have so much to talk about!'

Put that way, how could she refuse? Kathryn forced a smile, and, without looking at Rex, murmured, 'Oh, sure, that would be nice.'

'Good!' With a merry laugh, Flame led Derek away towards the steps. And almost before they were out of earshot, Rex drawled,

'Nice, Kate?' He grabbed Kathryn's nearest hand, curling her fingers within his large palm. 'Just nice? Didn't your English teachers in school tell you to avoid that word . . . to try to find one that's more descriptive?'

It felt wonderful to be walking with her hand in his. But she allowed herself to savour the delightful sensation for only a fraction of a second; anything more would have been too dangerous. Sliding her fingers free, she stuffed her hands safely into the pockets of her shorts.

'Nice?' She pretended to concentrate her attention on the pinky-white cliff to their left as they rounded the headland. 'What's wrong with nice?'

'It's ... boring, Kate.'

'So?'

'Touché!' He chuckled. 'OK, so you find me boring.' He swung an arm around her shoulders and pulled her against him, so that her hip brushed his thigh as she walked. 'I could have sworn, this morning in the pool, that the last things you were thinking of were "nice" and "boring".'

While she had spent time on the veranda with Derek, she had felt the sun flushing her cheeks; she hoped now that the rush of colour flooding her skin would be hidden under the beginnings of her tan. 'I wasn't thinking anything, this morning in the pool,' she retorted, 'for the simple reason that I was still half asleep.' A lie, of course ...

'Ah.' He chuckled. 'Then I can only dream about how much more passionate you would have been had you been fully awake—it positively boggles the mind ...'

'That's not what I meant ...' She realised she was blustering. She was also being foolish. There were no words to excuse or explain away what had happened between them in the pool.

The facts spoke for themselves. She decided it would be simpler to stop hedging, and face him straight on. 'You're a very sexy man, Rex. I doubt any woman with blood in her veins would have managed to resist your kiss, but——'

'Correct me if I'm wrong, Kate...but wasn't it...*your* kiss?'

Damn him! 'Oh, whatever!' she retorted, her shrug irritable. 'Must we talk about it? It happened, it's over...and as far as I'm concerned that's an end to it. Just one little kiss.' She made a derisive sound. 'It meant nothing...to me, at any rate.'

'Why are you lying to me, Kate?' There was a trace of genuine perplexity in his voice. 'Because you *are* lying...to me, if not to yourself.'

'What makes you think I'm lying?' Kathryn tilted her chin defiantly.

'It's a gift I have,' he said, with a tilted smile that twined another snare around her heart. 'One that has made me the successful journalist I am!'

'Well, you aren't being paid to give me the third degree,' she said primly. 'So can we just get on with our search for your darned shells, and then get back to the villa?'

'The shells.' Rex's eyes looked blank for a moment, as if he'd forgotten the reason for their walk. 'Oh, the shells.' He narrowed his eyes against the sun, and then, in a voice that held more than a trace of surprise, said, 'Good lord, the place is a treasure trove.'

Kathryn could see that indeed it was. Shells of many kinds littered the white sand; most of them looked as if they were intact.

Rex seemed to have forgotten her existence, as he walked here and there, picking up one shell after another, examining them, putting them down, shaking his head disbelievingly.

'Lord, look at that...' He picked his way past a pile of seaweed, and, bending down, lifted up a large shell.

Wandering after him, Kathryn felt her sandals sink into the fine grains of crushed coral. When she reached him, she saw that the shell was a pretty grey colour. He was turning it over curiously.

'What is it?' she asked.

'Mmm?' He turned to her vaguely, as if he'd forgotten about her for a moment. 'Oh. *Strombus gigas.*'

'*Strombus gigas*?' Her voice was questioning.

'A queen conch.'

'Do you have one? In your collection?'

'Mmm.' He traced a fingertip over the yellow, wavy lip. 'Yes, I do...but this one is a beauty. Why don't you take it home with you, as a keepsake?'

'No.' Despite the heat of the sun, and the perspiration that was making her shirt cling to her back, she felt a chill shiver down her spine. 'No...I...' She bit her lip. 'I...don't like shells.'

His eyes were very serious as he looked at her. 'You said last night that they were empty. Now you say you don't like them. My God, Kate, just look at this—look at the colouring— it's exquisite.' Lowering his gaze for a moment, he ran the tip of his middle finger inside the gleaming pink of the wide aperture. 'Look at the richness...'

'It's empty.' Her voice was as hollow and empty as the shell. She knew it, but could do nothing about it. He must think her crazy.

He didn't look as if he was thinking her crazy. He was holding the shell to his ear. 'Oh, it's not empty, Katie, my love.' He held it out, and before she could move back he held the shell to her ear. 'Listen...listen to the music of the sea. Close your eyes...'

So that he wouldn't see the pain there, she did close her eyes...but she closed her ears too. She didn't listen, didn't want to listen. But she couldn't shut out his words as he went on,

'Do you hear it, Kate, the music of the sea? And there's more than music, if you really listen. The shell isn't empty. It has a soul; listen, dream, and the beauty of it will touch your own.'

She exhaled frustratedly, and made an effort to listen, just so she could shut out his words...but she didn't hear music...not the music of the sea, or any other kind of music. And as for a soul...all she could hear was an angry whirring sound. A sound that became louder and angrier by the moment...

She frowned, and just then Rex drew the shell from her ear. But strangely she could still hear the whirring sound; only now it was so loud that it was almost deafening.

And all at once, she realised the noise had been coming not from the inner depths of the shell, but from the sky.

Squinting up against the sun, she saw the helicopter, making its descent to the landing-pad. And as she watched, the pilot set it down...and the angry noise began to fade away.

'Our transportation has arrived, Kate.' Rex's eyes held more than a trace of regret. 'It's time to be getting back.' Dropping the shell, he cupped his hand under her elbow, and then, after hesitating for a fraction of a second, he bent his head and brushed a gentle kiss on her brow.

'Yes,' she said quietly, 'it's time to go home.'

As they walked together back to the villa, she was swamped by a feeling of desolation so intense that she had to fight back the tears pricking the backs of her eyes.

She had said, 'It's time to go home.'

But she knew that because of the way things were, although the man at her side couldn't know it, what she'd really been saying was, 'It's time to say goodbye.'

CHAPTER NINE

'So ——' Trish Rice sauntered into Kathryn's office around nine o'clock on Monday morning '—how was your weekend?'

Kathryn was putting some papers away in her filing-cabinet; when she heard the secretary's voice, she pushed the metal drawer shut, before straightening and turning round.

Trish, she saw, was standing a few feet from the half-open door, one hand resting on her thin hip...but, despite her effort to appear languid, the eager light in her piggy eyes left Kathryn in no doubt as to her avid interest. Whatever the woman gleaned now, Kathryn knew, would be all over the office before the coffee break.

She smiled, an easy smile. 'Flame Cantrell is even more beautiful in the flesh than she is on screen.' There wasn't much Trish could do to twist *that* piece of news into some sordid morsel of gossip fit for the front page of some sleazy magazine.

'Oh, Flame Cantrell—who cares about her?' Trish shrugged irritably. 'What I want to know

187

is —— ' she licked her thin lips, and Kathryn decided wet worms mating would have looked more attractive '—*how* did you make out with our own pet Panther?'

'Make out?' Kathryn frowned, as if puzzled. 'What on earth do you mean . . . ?'

With an impatient exclamation, Trish said, 'You know . . . did he come on to you? When word filtered out that Charlie was sick and Rex had gone to the Caribbean with you . . . well, I mean, everybody's just been agog to know what happened!'

Kathryn yawned . . . and it wasn't entirely an act. Though the flight from Guadeloupe to Vancouver via Montreal had been smooth and—unlike the outward trip—without any hitches, it had been close to one in the morning before she and Rex had deplaned, and almost an hour later when Rex had dropped her off outside her apartment building. She had tumbled into bed, expecting to go out like a light, but her jumbled thoughts had kept her awake till about half an hour before her alarm went off. As a result, she felt utterly washed out; if it hadn't been for the light tan she'd acquired while at the villa, and a little more eye make-up than she usually wore, she knew she would be looking like death warmed up. Perhaps tonight she would sleep better . . .

'Well?'

She blinked as Trish's insistent voice broke into her musings.

'You want to know what happened?' Kathryn's taupe silk blouse rustled as she moved towards the door. With her eyes fixed steadily on Trish, she pulled the door wide open and said in a cool voice, 'If you want an answer to *that* question, why don't you go straight to the horse's mouth?'

Trish sniggered. 'To the panther's mouth, you mean. Well, I might just... Oh!' She broke off breathlessly as she caught sight of the tall male figure who had appeared in the doorway. 'Rex—good morning! I didn't see you there...'

Kathryn felt her throat muscles tighten as she looked at Rex... and had to squash an automatic impulse to smooth a hand over her chignon to reassure herself that there wasn't one blonde hair out of place; even if her hair had been as untidy as an old feather duster, why should she care if Rex Panther saw it? There would never be anything between them; there could never be anything between them.

She saw that his black eyebrows were quirked in question as he looked at Trish. 'Go to the panther's mouth for what?' he asked blandly.

'Oh—er—I was...er...'

'I . . . thought I heard you ask Kathryn what happened between the two of us over the weekend.' He turned his glance towards Kathryn for a second and, though she felt no sympathy for the other woman, the cold look now in his eye made her feel a little uneasy. What was he going to say?

'I think,' he went on, 'that neither Kate nor I would wish to talk about what happened between us. The simplest things can be exaggerated out of all recognition—in all innocence, of course—and, before you know it, rumours are flying and reputations are ruined. I'm sure you, Trish, would be the last person to wish that on Kate . . . or on me. Shall we just say a good time was had by all, and leave it at that?'

Though he spoke in a pleasant tone, there was no mistaking the hint of warning in his voice. He had made it quite clear he knew exactly what Trish was up to, and was letting her know that if she manufactured any gossip, and spread it around, he'd trace it right back to her. Kathryn saw a dark red colour seep up over Trish's pale face.

The secretary tossed back her head, and her brown hair swished over her shoulders. 'You don't have to worry,' she said stiffly as she made to leave, 'I have more important things to do than gossip about Kathryn Ashby. It's common knowledge anyway that she's nothing but a cold fish —— '

Rex's hand snaked out and caught her arm, halting her. 'You little bitch,' he said angrily. 'I'll have you know that Kate Ashby has more warmth in her little finger than you have in your whole body —— '

'Rex,' Kathryn interrupted, 'don't. It doesn't matter to me what Trish or anyone else thinks —— '

'No?' A nerve twitched below his right eye. 'Well, it matters one helluva lot to me. I won't stand by and hear you being maligned, especially by a vicious little —— '

'Oh, pardon me!' Trish jerked her arm away from his grip. 'And aren't *you* the perfect gallant knight? Well, you may have melted the Ice Woman with your New York ways and your big-city charm, but I'll have you know that you're not fooling some of us.' She tilted her chin scornfully as she turned to Kathryn. 'And I'll give you a tip, Ms High and Mighty Ashby—I'd keep well away from Rex Panther if I were you. They say that gentlemen prefer blondes...but the blonde woman *this* so-called gentleman has been seen around town with lately is a married lady!' And with that parting shot, before Rex could respond she sped away down the corridor, her brown hair flying out behind her.

Kathryn turned with a sigh and walked back into her office. Why had Rex had to turn up just then? She had been perfectly capable of handling Trish on her own. And in the past she'd managed to maintain at least a superficial veneer of civility with the other woman. Now it would be open warfare.

But one good thing had come out of the nasty little interlude: Trish had confirmed to her that there was indeed a lady in Rex's life. A blonde, if Trish were to be believed . . . and a married one to boot. Now *that* surprised her. Surely Rex Panther could have his pick of all the available women in Vancouver; but if so, then why would he get involved with someone who was married? But what did it matter to her? She felt the same amount of pain, whether the 'lady in his life' was single or not . . .

'Kate . . .' She heard Rex's voice right behind her, felt his warm breath on the sensitive skin at her nape. 'I think we need to talk. Take a break and let's go across the street for a coffee.'

She turned and wished she hadn't; the movement more or less had her ending up in his embrace. His arms seemed to go around her as naturally as if they were man and wife.

'I missed you last night,' he murmured in her ear. 'Who would have thought that spending nights with you would so quickly become habit-forming —— ?'

'Just one night,' she protested, keeping her eyes averted from his face.

'You're forgetting about our night on the plane, Katie.' His lips were nibbling her earlobe. 'You may have slept through that one, but I didn't.'

She had slept through that one...but she hadn't slept through the next one. She had tossed and turned, her body aching for him...just as it was beginning to ache now. She had to put a stop to it.

Jerkily, she moved out of his embrace, and walked round to the other side of her desk.

Lowering her gaze, she began shuffling some papers on her desk. 'I'm sorry, Rex, I've got a lot to do...'

'What's the matter?' His voice was rough. 'You're not letting what Trish said —— '

'It has nothing to do with anything Trish said.' With an effort, she raised her eyes and looked at him again. 'I'm not denying that I...had fun with you on the weekend. But that's over now. As far as I'm concerned, it was just that...fun. And now it's back to work. As I told you before, the only thing I have room for in my life is my career. I have neither the time nor the inclination for emotional entanglements.'

Just as she finished speaking her phone rang. Thankful of the excuse to focus her mind elsewhere, she picked up the receiver.

'Kathryn, it's Ken here. Is Rex there, by any chance? I've been trying to track him down.'

'Yes, he's here. Do you want to talk with him?'

'Not on the phone. Tell him to come to my office. Thanks.'

Kathryn replaced the handset. 'That was for you,' she said. 'Ken wants you to go to his office.'

'Kate...' Rex came forward, and, placing his palms on her desk, leaned towards her, his eyes serious. 'I'd like to see you tonight. I've already made plans for dinner, but I'll come round and pick you up after...'

Yes, she knew he already had plans for dinner. Hadn't she overheard him arranging to meet with Laura, the lady in his life? Resentment mingled with the pain slashing through her; what kind of man was he, that he would go from one woman to another on the same evening? Only this awareness of his duplicity made it possible for her to withstand the seductive, burning intensity in his black-lashed amber eyes.

'I'm going to be working tonight, at home. I promised Ken he'd have the first prints on his desk tomorrow.' She gazed at him steadily. 'I'm sorry, Rex.'

He quirked an eyebrow. 'Tomorrow, then?'

'I'm going to be pretty busy for the rest of the week . . . but thanks anyway.'

Rex straightened. 'Don't think I'm put off so easily, Kate Ashby.' His lips curved in a smile that would have torn her heart in two if she'd let it. 'I have to go now . . . but I'll be stepping up my campaign. You know what they say: faint heart never won fair lady. And you're one fair lady I intend to win.'

Whistling softly, he turned and walked away. He didn't look back. And as he closed the door behind him, Kathryn felt herself slumping down in her chair. How many fair ladies did he want in his life? she wondered dully. And how many did he think he could cope with at a time?

Well, be it two or ten, or ten times ten, it didn't matter to her. She had no intention of letting herself be one of them.

She hadn't been lying about what she'd been planning to do that evening, and right after dinner she went through to her darkroom, a large converted closet in her apartment.

Usually, she loved being in there. Loved the peace of it, loved the feeling of isolation, loved the familiar smell of the chemicals ... and most of all she loved the feeling of satisfaction she got when she saw the end-product of her creative endeavours. From the time she was a little girl, her father, a keen amateur photographer, had encouraged her to help him develop and print the pictures he took, and the process had fascinated her from the word go. Transferring the prints from tray to tray, watching the images form on the paper—it had been like magic to her...

But this evening, as she developed the first rolls of film she'd shot on the island, working quickly and carefully as always in the pale glow of the red bulb, she found that her thoughts kept drifting away from the task at hand.

Drifting to Rex Panther.

After he'd left her office, she hadn't seen him again all day, but she'd kept herself so busy that she hadn't had time to miss him. Hadn't had time to think about him. But she was certainly making up for it now!

With a sigh, she glanced at her watch. Lord, it was half-past eleven! She hung the first of the prints on the line to dry, and, putting up one hand to cover a yawn, switched out the light with the other. It was time, she thought, to call it a night. Not only had she the beginnings of a headache, she felt bone-weary. Thank heavens she hadn't felt this dreadful lassitude when she was down in the Caribbean; every cell in her body seemed to crave sleep. She had intended to have a shower once she finished the job at hand, but she'd have to forgo that. All she wanted to do was crawl into her bed and go to sleep!

Tomorrow, when she went in to the office, she would decide what she was going to do. And depending upon how often she thought she was going to be thrown together with Rex Panther in the future, she would make up her mind whether or not to quit her job at the *Clarion*.

To love him, knowing she must deny herself that love, was already more than she could bear.

She didn't, however, go to the office the following day. When her alarm went off at six-thirty, she discovered that the way she'd felt the night before hadn't just been the effects of jet-lag; she had obviously been coming down with something. And the something had arrived...in full force. Her slight headache had become one of major proportions, every bone in her body ached, her eyes were sore and gritty, and when she tried to swallow her throat felt as if someone had been ramming great shards of broken glass down it while she was asleep.

She spluttered, and groaned, and then, fumbling for the button on the alarm clock, switched it off. Almost knocking over the bedside lamp as she put it on, she scrabbled for the phone. Ken wouldn't be in yet, but she would leave a message on his tape. She'd told him yesterday that she'd have the first pictures for the Flame Cantrell spread on his desk today; she decided that if she made a supreme effort she could get up in a little while and package them.

She left her message on his tape, hoping he could interpret her hoarse, strained words. 'I'm taking the day off, Ken. Send over a courier for the pictures ... I'll have them ready by noon.'

But the moment she put the receiver back on its cradle, she flopped back on the pillow, forgetting all about Ken, all about the pictures, all about everything.

And she must have fallen asleep, for she dreamed.

She dreamed that she was back on L'Ile des Coquilles with Rex Panther. He was dragging her along the sand below the villa, back to the

Bay of Shells, and once he got her there he held huge conches to her ear, one after the other.

Listen, Kate, he ordered her. Listen to the music. Listen to the soul. Listen. Listen. Listen.

His face grew sad when she tried to pull away...but there was a spark of anger too. Finally, when she thought she could stand no more, he took the largest conch and banged it against her ear. Over and over again, till the pain and the noise were unbearable.

Listen, listen, listen!

Stop it, stop it, stop it! she shouted. Go away! Leave me alone! Can't you see...I don't *want* to listen!

But the hammering went on, and on, and on, till she could stand it no more...

No! she shouted. And as she did, the sound of her own voice, raised in protest, jerked her awake. Groggily, as she tried to separate dream from reality, she raised her head from the pillow and listened.

Oh, lord, she groaned as she sank back on to the pillow again. There was someone at the door. Battering and banging...

She glanced blearily at the alarm clock, and moaned when she saw it was almost noon. It must be the courier, come for the pictures.

She ran the tip of her tongue over her parched lips, and, as she tried to swallow, again felt the burning rawness in her throat. She would have to get up; she would have to tell the courier she didn't have the package ready...and she would have to phone Ken to apologise.

With every bone protesting, she twisted herself to a sitting position. Her nightgown, she realised, was clinging to her as if it was damp. She plucked the yoke away from her chest and felt the fabric between her fingers. It was more than damp, she thought distantly, it was soaking wet.

She shivered as she got out of bed, and, despite the warmth of the central heating, she felt goose-bumps rise on her arms as she slipped into her blue silk robe.

She had two deadbolts on her door, and with her fingers slippy from perspiration it must have taken her a full thirty seconds to get them open. Gathering the collar of her robe around her neck with one shaking hand, she opened the door with the other...and it wasn't till the door was open, and she saw the tall figure looking down at her, that she realised she had forgotten to look through the peep-hole to check the caller's identity. Blame it on the flu, she thought in some distant part of her mind...

'For God's sake!' Rex Panther had the same anger in his eyes as he'd had in her dream. But he had no conch in his hand—what he had was a huge black umbrella, and it was dripping with rain.

Incey-Wincey spider crawled up the water spout,
Down came the rain and washed the spider out...

The words of the old rhyme echoed dizzily in Kathryn's head. She moved back and leaned against the edge of the sofa table as he came in, and when he slammed the door behind him her hand went involuntarily to her temple in protest as the sound reverberated in her head.

'So,' she said, her voice so raspy that she scarcely recognised it, 'what do you want?'

Perhaps it was the lingering effect of her dream, perhaps it was the persistent, gnawing suspicion that Trish was right and he was involved with a married woman... or perhaps it was because he was seeing her now at her worst—she didn't need to look in a mirror to know that her eyes were red, her face drawn and pale, her hair as straggly as if she'd just crawled through a hedge backwards—but, whatever the reason, she found herself on the offensive.

'I happened to be in Ken's office,' he said tersely, 'when he listened to your message on his tape. You sounded ghastly, and I wanted to check up on you...so I offered to call by at noon for the pictures——'

'They're not ready.' Kathryn had meant the words to come out haughtily, but instead they came out in a croak...and as she croaked, she started to cough...and once she started she couldn't seem to stop. With a choked out 'Excuse me!' she stumbled across to her small kitchen, and, reaching for the tap, ran the cold water. Shivering, she opened the cupboard door above the stove, but before she could take out a glass Rex got there.

He half filled a tall glass with water, and raised it to her lips. 'Here.'

With an irritable twitch of her shoulders, she took the glass from him, and turned her back on him while she drank. She could feel tears running down her cheeks, brought on by the coughing spell, and, after putting the glass on the countertop, she dug into the pocket of her robe for a Kleenex, and wiped the tears from her face.

She kept her back to him. 'Now,' she said, in a hoarse, strained voice, 'will you please leave and let me get back to bed?'

'Do you have someone to look after you?'

'I'm perfectly able to look after myself.'

'Don't be an idiot, Kate. Let's get you back to bed, and then I'll make you a hot drink. Here...' She heard the rustle of paper, and in the shiny surface of the black fridge she saw his reflection, saw him pull a small white bag from the pocket of his leather jacket. 'I dropped by the chemist and brought you a selection of goodies. Aspirin, some vitamin C tablets...'

Kathryn felt her knees begin to wobble dangerously; in another minute, she knew, she would begin to crumple, would end up making an absolute fool of herself.

'I don't believe in taking pills if I don't have to,' she said. 'So would you please —— ?'

'Kate —— ' his hands grasped her shoulders and he made her turn to face him '——just go to bed and at least... Good lord!' His expression changed, and his brows came down heavily. 'Your robe is soaking! Look, take this off and —— '

'I don't want your help!' she rasped.

'Lady, you are the most exasperating woman on the face of this earth. Your sheets must be soaking too. Tell me where you keep your linen and I'll change your bed.'

Kathryn knew it was now or never. Her legs were beginning to feel like wet string.

She curved her fingers—fingers which were shaking as if she had malaria—around the edge of the countertop behind her. 'Which part of the word "no" is it that you don't understand, Mr Panther?' Not only her fingers were trembling—her voice had trembled too; her whole body was trembling. And not only that, but she could feel tears begin to well up in her eyes; but through them, she stared at him defiantly, belligerently.

He stared back at her, for a long moment. The tension between them was so tight that Kathryn could almost feel the air throbbing with it, as it would throb to the beat of an eagle's wings. Then, with a sigh of utter frustration, Rex tossed the white bag on the table.

'Suit yourself,' he said, rubbing the back of his neck wearily. And with that he turned and walked away. For the first time since she'd known him, his shoulders weren't straight and arrogant; they slumped as if admitting defeat.

Kathryn waited till he clicked the door of the apartment shut behind him before she stumbled across the room, clutching at the back of the sofa to support herself as she almost fell. And after sliding the deadbolts shut, she made for the linen cupboard.

Five minutes later, she was back in bed again. But even in her warmest flannel nightgown, with fresh sheets on the bed and two extra blankets on top of her, she couldn't stop shivering.

Stubborn fool, she chastised herself, as she tried in vain to stop her teeth from chattering. Why hadn't she let the man help her?

But she knew the answer only too well. He had already stolen her heart; she had to make sure he didn't also steal her soul.

She was off work for the rest of the week— and the whole of the following week too. It had been a very bad flu, and it left her weak and debilitated. She had managed, however, to get the Cantrell prints finished during her first weekend at home, and she'd couriered them to Ken on the Monday. Apart from that, she had no contact with the office, other than calling Ken on the second Friday to tell him she was feeling much better and she'd be in after the weekend...and then, that same day, she phoned Charlie.

After they'd chatted for a few minutes, she said, in a deliberately casual voice, 'So, Charlie...did Rex fill you in on our trip to the Caribbean?'

'Haven't seen him, Kathryn. He's taken a couple of weeks off.'

Kathryn fiddled with the telephone coil at her end of the line. 'Have you ever met his wife?' She grimaced as she spoke, hating herself for being so devious. What did she expect to find out by asking a question to which she already knew the answer?

'He's not married. He's got a woman stashed away somewhere, though.' Charlie chuckled. 'Could you imagine a guy with as much going for him who wouldn't be involved? Apparently there's some cute little blonde in his life who's been complaining she didn't see enough of him. That's one of the reasons he's taking this break.'

What Charlie was saying only confirmed what Kathryn had already deduced for herself; Rex Panther had only been amusing himself with her. She had read far more into his actions than had really been there. Oh, she really had made a prize fool of herself, hadn't she?

Perhaps, she mused miserably, the time *had* come for her to leave the *Clarion* ... and to leave Vancouver. To look for a job with a paper back East again. She'd left Halifax only to get a complete change of scene after her breakup with Derek ... and at the time had intended the move to be just a temporary one. But she'd soon grown to love the West Coast—the changing seasons, the beautiful scenery, the closeness to rain forest and Pacific Ocean. It would be a wrench to leave all that behind...

But, she decided, ignoring the heavy ache in the region of her heart, that seemed to be the only course open to her, in the circumstances.

She wouldn't, though, give in her notice right away; she wouldn't want Rex to realise her leaving had anything to do with him. She'd wait a few weeks and then she'd have a talk with Ken—ask him if he'd any connections in Halifax in the newspaper world.

Getting up from her chair, she wandered across to the window, and, leaning her shoulder against the wall, looked out at the scene before her. Her apartment was situated just off West Georgia Street, close to the entrance to Stanley Park. From her window, which faced north-west, she could see Lost Lagoon. Today, she noticed, the waters glistened in the afternoon sun. Sliding open the patio doors leading to her balcony, she stepped outside. Even though snow still capped the twin peaks of the Lions, the air at this lower altitude was warm and balmy, and held the scents of spring.

It felt good, after she'd been cooped up inside for so long. Impulsively, she stepped back into the living-room again and closed the door, before making for her bedroom. There, she rummaged in her closet for one of her

jogging outfits. A run around Lost Lagoon—
a gentle run, since her legs still felt a bit
shaky—would be the best medicine for the way
she was feeling.

At least, she thought wryly as she pulled a
loose yellow sweatshirt over her purple Spandex
tights, it couldn't possibly make her feel worse!

CHAPTER TEN

BY SUNDAY, she was feeling back to normal.

And she had made a decision—a decision that had not come easily, but, after many hours of struggling with her conscience, seemed to be one she had to make.

She had to apologise to Rex Panther.

And she had to do it today. She had to do it this evening. Abstractedly, she stared at the silver-grey carpet on her living-room floor as she completed the stretching exercises she always did before her evening run around the park. When she went in to work in the morning, she didn't want to have to face him with the memory of her ungracious behaviour hanging like a black cloud over her head.

'Which part of the word "no" is it that you don't understand, Mr Panther?'

She blew out a self-deprecatory oath as she recalled the words she'd flung at him...and the contemptuous tone in which they'd been delivered. You would have thought, for heaven's sake, that the man had been attempting to rape her, instead of offering to nurse her. He had taken time out of his day to call by; he'd even been thoughtful enough to go to the chemist first, to buy medicine that might soothe her aches and cool her fever. But she had been too stubborn, too pigheaded, even to say 'Thank you'.

So—she touched her fingertips to the carpet one last time before straightening—if she was going to apologise, she had better do it now, before she chickened out.

As she walked to the phone in the kitchen, she realised her palms were slick with nervous perspiration. Rubbing them against her pink nylon shorts, she shook her head. She wasn't going to see the man, she was only going to talk to him on the phone . . .

But as she riffled through the pages of the phone book to get his number, the print seemed to run together. And when she eventually found his number, and dialled it, she could feel her heart thumping as if she'd just run a four-minute mile. Relax, she told herself tautly—just say what you have to say and hang up.

It took so long for someone to answer that she was beginning to think no one would. And the cowardly part of her was just about to express itself with a sigh of relief, when she heard a click. The dialling tone stopped. And she heard a throat being cleared at the other end of the line.

'Panther residence.'

Kathryn felt herself freeze. *A woman's voice.* Soft and feminine, it had an attractive built-in chuckle. But even as Kathryn noted this in a distant corner of her mind, she felt a strange, wobbly sensation in the pit of her stomach. It had never occurred to her that anyone but Rex himself would reply. Was it because, on that morning on the way to the airport he'd said, 'The place is empty,' that she'd somehow assumed that it would *always* be empty? How utterly ridiculous...

'Hello?' The female voice coming over the line had a slight edge to it now. 'Hello? Who's calling?'

Kathryn closed her eyes. All of a sudden her resolution dissipated like dew under a scorching sun; she could no sooner talk to Rex Panther now than she could have flown to the moon. Her apology would have to——

'Who is it, Laura? Someone for me?'

As Rex's voice, his familiar deep voice, sounded in the background Kathryn felt her heart give a great lurch. Stifling a panicky exclamation, with a hasty 'Sorry, wrong number' she jerked the phone from her ear as if it had suddenly become a dangerous weapon. With her teeth digging into her lower lip, she clattered the receiver back on to its cradle, keeping it pressed there with both hands as if expecting the man himself to materialise from the earpiece, like a genie out of a bottle, if she didn't.

What a wishy-washy fool she was! She felt like screaming with frustration, frustration at her own immature behaviour. Why couldn't she have calmly asked to speak to Rex, then just as calmly apologised for having been so ungrateful for his offer to help, before finishing off with an equally calmly spoken 'See you tomorrow, then'?

The only thing for which she could be thankful was that there was no way he could know she had ever called.

But *she* knew.

And as she jogged around the Stanley Park sea-wall half an hour later, she was still flagellating herself mentally for the way she'd acted. What was the matter with her? she wondered, slowing her pace as she approached the Teahouse Restaurant at Ferguson Point. No matter in what direction she tried to point her thoughts, they always came back to Rex Panther.

Panting a little, she jogged past the car park. It was a lovely, breezy evening, and the vehicles, she noted, were crammed together. The

Teahouse was a favourite dining spot for Vancouverites, the cuisine being excellent, and the view of the water stunning. Several groups of people were making their way from the car park to the restaurant's entrance.

Kathryn paused, jogging in place, as a tour bus went by. As she started to run again, slowly, her eye was caught by a glimpse of bright colour, and as she turned her head she saw a fair-haired woman in a peacock-blue dress walking along the path to the restaurant. She was laughing, obviously at something her companion had just said—a man with hair as black as charcoal and wearing a teal-blue blazer and beige trousers, a man with the same lean, rangy build as Rex Panther.

No—Kathryn felt panic clutch her heart— he didn't have the same lean, rangy build as Rex Panther.

It *was* Rex Panther.

Feeling as if an invisible hand had nailed her to the spot, Kathryn found herself standing stock-still, staring after them. But that was all right—there was no way he would notice her; he had his back to her, and they were walking towards the restaurant. As she watched, however, the woman paused, rubbing her hands over her bare arms as if she was cold, and she raised her face to Rex, and said something.

Kathryn couldn't hear what she said, but a moment later, after escorting his companion to the entrance, Rex turned and started striding back along the path. Along the path to the car park. Had he forgotten something? Had the woman sent him back for something? With a desperate sense of urgency, Kathryn's gaze darted from car to car, hoping to see the dented black Chevelle, hoping he wouldn't be coming in her direction. But there was no sign of the ancient vehicle; all the cars were shiny and new-looking...

Oh, dear God, he was walking towards her. Frowning, his expression absent, he obviously hadn't seen her yet.

Damn, damn, damn! Would it be better to stand stock-still and hope he wouldn't notice her...or start running...?

But as she glanced round frantically for a van or a bus behind which she could hide, she realised it was too late. He had spotted her.

Feeling her legs turn weak, she leaned against the body of the silver Mercedes beside her, hoping the owner wasn't watching from the restaurant.

'Well, good evening.' Rex halted in front of her, one hand in the pocket of his trousers. His jaw, she noted, was freshly shaven, his black hair brushed back, though the natural wave still fought to have its own way. His shirt was the finest of cotton and oyster-white; his tie was pure silk and two shades deeper than his eyes...eyes which at this moment were narrowed as they skimmed over her slender figure, which was so scantily clad in her brief pink shorts and her clinging Lycra T-shirt.

'Oh...hi.' Kathryn felt goose-bumps rise on every inch of her skin...both the covered, and the uncovered; there seemed, in her own mind, to be so much more of the latter. She decided she'd never in her life felt so underdressed.

'Are you...waiting for me?' His voice was cool but she could hear him jingle the keys in his pocket, the only clue to a restlessness which belied his appearance of calm self-control.

'Waiting for you?' Confused, Kathryn just stared at him.

He jerked his head towards the Mercedes. 'I thought you'd spotted my car and —— '

'This is your car?' Kathryn straightened and hurriedly moved a step away from it. 'I didn't know this was your car.'

He drew his hand from his pocket, along with the keys which he'd been jingling. 'It's mine. I have two cars. One for work —— ' he unlocked the front door at the passenger side, where she was standing, and drew out a black mohair stole which had been draped over the back of the seat '——and one for play.' As he clicked the door shut, the scent of Lancôme's Trésor drifted to Kathryn's nostrils from the stole, faintly, yet it was strong enough to overpower the fragrance from the blue hyacinths in the flowerbeds near by.

'I thought —— ' his eyes were enigmatic as he continued '——that when you changed your mind about talking to me on the phone you'd somehow discovered I was coming here for dinner, and you planned to waylay me. What was it that couldn't wait till tomorrow?'

Kathryn stared up at him. 'How on earth did you know it was...?' She grimaced. He could only have been guessing she was the one who'd been on the other end of the line; now, however, she'd given herself away. 'Oh,' she said flatly, 'you were just guessing.'

'No, it wasn't a lucky guess.' He kept staring at her, and she felt more uncomfortable by the moment. 'I have one of those devices that notes the origin of every incoming call.' His lips twisted in a mocking smile that let her know he was well aware that this possibility had never occurred to her. 'Everything considered, you're the last person I'd have expected to be calling me, Miss Ashby.'

Miss Ashby. She felt something inside her give a little cry of protest. So... no more Kate, no more Katie. Everything between them was to be formal from now on.

She wanted to hang her head, and stare at the ground. Instead she fixed her gaze on a point an inch to the right of his head. 'I called to apologise for being so rude when you came round on Tuesday.' She felt her throat muscles tighten, and when she went on her voice was husky. 'I'm sorry.'

'Oh.' His tone seemed warmer, or was she just imagining it? 'Apology accepted——'

'Rex, honey...' A woman's voice broke into his words, and involuntarily Kathryn turned in the direction of the sound. Coming towards them, along the path from the restaurant, was the woman in the peacock-blue dress. In one fleeting glance, Kathryn took in every detail of her appearance—the long ash-blonde hair, the Grace Kelly features, the slim figure so elegantly draped in raw silk...and the lovely eyes which were fixed on her with interest and curiosity...eyes the dreamy blue of a robin's egg.

Kathryn had walked into the glass door of a patio once, and now she felt the same sense of pain and shock. This was the woman she'd seen the morning she and Rex flew to the Caribbean, when she'd wandered along Rex's street in the snow. The woman who lived in the Cape Cod house. The woman with the husband, the station wagon . . . and the three children.

Rex Panther—Trish *had* been right, and seeing the proof sucked the breath from her lungs as she tried to assimilate that proof—was having an affair with a married woman.

'Well,' she stuttered, 'I must be going. I hope,' she added in a voice so high-pitched that she didn't recognise it, 'that you have a nice dinner.' No, it wouldn't be just 'nice', she thought hysterically. 'Nice' meant 'boring', and no dinner with Rex Panther could ever be boring——

'Wait, Kate . . .'

'Sorry, got to go!'

And with that she was off, barely hearing the screech of brakes, the obscenity screamed at her by a cab driver as she ran into the road and he swerved to avoid her.

Along the seawall she pounded, mile after mile after mile, the pounding of her feet echoing the heavy pounding of her heart, till her breath was coming so painfully, so raggedly that she could go no further, and she found herself bent over double at the edge of the path, gasping for air.

And while she stood there, on grass so green that it was dazzling to the eye, she realised that the decision she'd made—the decision to leave

Vancouver because she was in love with Rex Panther—was no longer valid. She would not leave Vancouver, and she would not leave the *Clarion*.

Now that she knew what kind of a man he was, she could no longer feel the same way about him.

Rex was, in his own way, just as flawed as Derek.

She would take back her heart—she should never have relinquished it in the first place— and lock it up so that she would never, *ever* be tempted to give it again.

The good weather continued throughout the next week. The TV weatherman was predicting that March was going to break all records for hours of sunshine. Kathryn was hardly in the office at all, having been assigned to take the photographs for a feature on transportation for tourists, which necessitated, among other things, taking a trip up the Sunshine Coast on one of the BC Ferries, and a trip from the mainland to Vancouver Island on another, and a return trip on the Sealink, the catamaran which ran between downtown Vancouver and downtown Victoria. Once again, Charlie was her partner, and, with his irrepressible sense of humour, he made what was an extremely exhausting week also an enjoyable one.

They had used his car to get from one place to another, and after arriving back at Horseshoe Bay just before three on the Friday afternoon he had driven her home.

'No point in going in to the office at this time on a Friday,' he'd grinned. 'Ken will just think of something else for us to do.' He pulled in at the kerb outside her apartment building, and as she unfastened her seatbelt he added, 'Oh, hey—I almost forgot! When I phoned Emma from Nanaimo, she said to invite you for dinner. Nothing fancy, but she guessed you'd be too pooped to cook tonight. How about it?'

Kathryn hesitated for only a moment—just long enough to picture her lonely apartment, with nothing in the fridge but a few cartons of yoghurt and some carrots. The thought of going out for groceries, when she felt so weary that all she wanted to do was sink into a hot bath, made up her mind for her.

'Sounds great, Charlie.' She slipped out of her seat and stepped on to the pavement. Holding the door open, she leaned into the car and said, 'I'll bring the wine.'

'Good girl. See you around seven? The kids'll be in bed ... We'll sit back and relax.'

With a smile, Kathryn clicked shut the door, and as Charlie pulled his Volvo from the kerb she walked slowly towards the entrance of her building. Her camera gear, she decided with a weary sigh as she heaved the strap higher on her shoulder, had never felt heavier.

It would be a good idea, she mused as she walked up the flight of steps leading to the front door, to take a cab to Charlie's. That way, if she had a couple of glasses of wine with dinner, she wouldn't have to worry about driving home.

She heard her phone ringing as she unlocked her apartment door.

Dropping her equipment on the nearest chair, she hurried to the kitchen to answer it, leaning against the fridge as she did.

'Hi!' Her voice was slightly breathless. 'Kathryn Ashby here...'

'Ah, Kate.'

She closed her eyes. Did the man have ESP? How could he have known she was just coming in the door?

'I've been trying to get you for the past hour...'

Her lips twisted in a wry smile. Good. No ESP...just perseverance.

'What's the matter?' she asked, her steady voice giving no indication of the tipsy way her heartbeats were hopping around.

'I was wondering if you were free tonight.'

Kathryn found herself staring into the sink; a small black spider was scuttling around as if looking for a way out. Automatically, she turned on the cold tap and watched the water wash the little creature down the drain.

'Kate? Are you still there?'

'Yes. I'm here.' Faint heart, he had said once, never won fair lady. Certainly no one could accuse him of being faint-hearted. Fickle-hearted, though...

A picture formed in her head of Rex at the Teahouse with that woman. With...*Laura*. Why was it she found it so difficult just to *think* the name? Rex and Laura at the Teahouse. Rex and Laura in his Shaugnessy home. Rex and Laura on the phone when he was at Flame Cantrell's villa. 'I'm sorry,' she said quietly. 'I'm not free tonight. I've already made plans.'

'Plans?' There was the faintest hint of disbelief in his tone.

'I'm having dinner with Charlie and his wife.'

'Mmm.'

She wouldn't have believed anyone could express doubt with such a small sound. 'Obviously,' she snapped, 'you think I'm lying.

Why would I? If I didn't want to go out with you, why wouldn't I just say so? But the fact is, I am going to Charlie's ... and if you don't believe me, why don't you just give him a call? Goodbye!'

Slamming down the phone, she staggered through to the bedroom. Throwing off her jacket, she tossed it on to the bed, and made for the bathroom. A long, long, hot bath was what she needed.

She poured bubble bath with an extravagant hand under the gushing tap, and, feeling as if she'd been run over by a bus, she unbuttoned her silk blouse, slipped it off, unzipped her linen skirt, let it fall to the floor, and then divested herself of her tights and undies with the very last remnants of her energy.

The water looked and felt like sea-green velvet. Sleek, caressing, luxurious.

Letting her head fall back on to the cushioned plastic pillow, she closed her eyes and let every bit of tension seep from her body.

And every last thought of Rex Lothario Panther seep from her mind.

'Piat d'Or?' Emma looked at the label on the wine bottles Kathryn had handed her as she came in. 'Wonderful!' Thanks so much.' She put the brown paper bag on the hall table and gave Kathryn an exuberant hug. 'Lovely to see you—it's been ages, hasn't it?'

'Mmm.' Kathryn slipped off her short cerise jacket, and hung it in the hall closet. 'You're looking well, Emma. All rested up after the family bout with measles?'

Emma rolled her huge chocolate-brown eyes. 'I wouldn't want to go through that again in a hurry.' Her drawled words were accompanied by a lazy smile. Tall and very slim, she was wearing an ankle-length rib-knit outfit in a strange shade of orange that did wonders for her. She stood back, and let her gaze skim over Kathryn's black dress. 'Well, don't *you* look stunning! I'd kill for a dress like that—where on earth did you find it?'

'My mother bought it in New York—she and my dad went down there for Christmas.'

'You've lost a little weight—probably that flu you had.' Emma looped an arm through one of Kathryn's as she led her through to the living-room. It always surprised Kathryn that Charlie, such a down-to-earth and homely type, should have wooed and won a woman like Emma; they were so different. But they absolutely doted on each other, and Emma had been more than happy to give up her career as a fashion designer to stay home and bring up their three children.

'There'll be lots of time for me later, once the kids are able to look after themselves,' she had said once, when Kathryn had asked her if she didn't miss the glitz and glamour of the fashion world.

Now, as they walked along the hall, which was beautifully appointed with fine mahogany furniture, Emma said to Kathryn in a whisper, 'I hope you don't mind, but Charlie invited someone else to join us. You could have knocked me down with a feather when he accepted... We've asked him before, but...'

As she spoke, she opened the French doors leading to the living-room, and, standing back, signalled to Kathryn to go ahead. With an unsuspecting smile on her face, Kathryn passed through the open doorway, into the familiar living-room, where a leaping fire glowed in the marble hearth, and the Chinese carpet gave a feeling of luxurious comfort, as did the rich cream and gold fabric covering the upholstered furniture.

Charlie was standing over by the drinks table, dressed in a green polo shirt and a pair of casual khaki trousers. He turned with a word of cheery greeting when he saw Kathryn, but after that first, astonished second her eyes were not for him...

They were for the man standing at the hearth, with his back to the fire. Facing her. The man in the black suit and black turtle-neck, the man with his hands resting easily in his pockets, the man with the teasing twinkle in his eyes as he watched her approach.

'Hi, Charlie.' Kathryn summoned all the self-control of which she was capable. Ordering the muscles around her mouth to move her lips into a smile, she said, allowing just the right amount of careless surprise to show in her tone, 'Why— Rex.' She hesitated...but in the end couldn't resist. 'How very...*nice*...to see you.'

'Wonderful to see you too.' The corners of his mouth twitched.

'What'll you have, Kathryn?' Charlie crossed the room and gave Rex a glass of sparkling liquid. 'Your ginger ale, sir!'

'I think...a rye and Seven, Charlie.' She needed one good stiff one to carry her over this first part of the evening.

'Sit down, Kathryn.' Emma gestured towards the sofa by the fire, and Kathryn crossed the room and sat down. 'As I was saying, Kathryn —— ' Emma moved across the room to join her husband '——just after Charlie came home, Rex happened to call him, to ask how your trip went. Since he was going to be alone this evening, Charlie asked him to come over and join us for dinner. I've warned them both there's to be no shop talk.' She ruffled her husband's hair, and he grinned.

Kathryn sensed Rex's eyes on her, but she kept hers averted; she knew as well as he that with just a few words she could reveal to Charlie and Emma just how underhanded he'd been—but, knowing her hosts the way she did, she also guessed they'd think it very amusing. Besides, she didn't want them to learn that Rex had asked her out; she didn't want them—or anyone else—to think there was anything going on between them.

'Where did you park, Kathryn?' Charlie had drawn back the curtains and was looking down into the front drive. 'Is your car out on the street, beside Rex's?'

'I took a cab. I thought I'd have some wine with dinner, and drinking and driving is no longer an option.'

'Wise girl.' That was Rex. 'But no point in spending money on a cab. I'll drive you home.'

No way! 'Oh, I wouldn't dream of letting you——'

'Don't be silly, Kathryn!' Emma came across with Kathryn's drink. 'Rex goes right by your place.'

There was a little silence as they all looked at her...and she knew Emma was right. Emma and Charlie lived on the North Shore, and Rex had to drive past her apartment on his way home. She would look utterly foolish if she turned him down.

'Of course.' Kathryn managed a bright smile as she took the glass from Emma. 'Thanks, Rex, I appreciate your offer. Very... nice... of you.'

It may have been nice of him, but the thought of being alone with him in his car for the drive home totally ruined her evening... an evening that had been spoiled anyway, from the moment she'd seen him standing at the fire.

Why on earth had he gone to the bother of inveigling himself into the Burke household for dinner? Oh, it was obviously because he'd known she'd be there... but why did he want to see her? He already had a woman in his life... a woman far more beautiful than she, and one about whom he was obviously serious. But, of course, *Laura* was married...

As Kathryn sipped her drink slowly, only half listening to the conversation around her, a sudden thought slithered into her head, one that outraged her so much that she almost gasped aloud. Was he wanting to use her as a decoy? Was he hoping that if he flaunted her as his lover the world in which he moved would be blinded to the fact that she, Kathryn Ashby, was only a cover?

The thought, which had seemed so far-out at first, took on more depth and credibility as they ate dinner; Rex was extremely attentive, so much so that she felt herself become hot with embarrassment . . . and she was sure she saw Emma and Charlie exchanging delighted glances.

She chose to resume the same seat in the living-room after dinner, and felt irritated when Rex chose to sit beside her. After a few minutes, he ran his arm casually along the sofa back, and though he never actually touched her during the course of the evening his closeness drove her crazy. She tried silently willing him to move, but he didn't budge an inch. At least, not till around ten, when he got to his feet abruptly. Thank heavens, Kathryn uttered a silent prayer of thanks, he was going to go sit elsewhere.

But instead, he said, 'Well, folks, I think it's time to call it a night. Charlie's been stifling yawns for the past half-hour . . . and Kate here's not much better. So, if you don't mind, we'll just get our coats and be on our way.'

Even if Kathryn had felt like protesting, she couldn't have. Charlie's rueful smile, his white face, revealed more than words just how weary he was.

'You're right, Rex,' he grinned, putting his arm around Emma's shoulders. 'I just can't take it any more. When I hit the big 4-0, it was as if I started going downhill on a toboggan! I just can't stand late nights at all.'

Kathryn got to her feet. She'd had only two drinks all evening—the rye before dinner, and one glass of white wine with Emma's delicious chicken casserole—so she couldn't blame alcohol for the dizziness in her head, for the tension and excitement throbbing through her. There had been something singing between herself and Rex since the moment their eyes had locked when she'd arrived . . .

And she knew, deep in her heart, that, no matter what happened between them tonight, things were never going to be the same for her again.

CHAPTER ELEVEN

REX must have realised she was in no mood for small talk, because he spoke not one word during the drive back from Charlie's. The traffic wasn't particularly heavy, so she knew he couldn't be concentrating on that as the Mercedes skimmed across the Lions Gate Bridge and along the Stanley Park Causeway. Perhaps he sensed the turmoil of her feelings, perhaps he noticed the hands clenched tensely in her lap, perhaps he'd seen the private, angry glance she'd shot him as he'd helped her on with her jacket. Whatever the reason, it wasn't till he'd drawn the car to a halt by the kerb at her apartment building that he finally spoke.

'Would you like to make me a cup of coffee?' There was a slight raspiness in his voice that made it very sexy.

'No.' She clasped her hands together primly and stared straight ahead. 'I would not.'

'I'm not asking you to make love.' His amusement was showing at the edges. 'Just coffee.'

She could have sworn she heard a little crack, as if, with his quick sense of humour, he'd chipped away a corner of her shell. There was something about him that, despite the way he seemed to rub her the wrong way, still managed to get under her skin. Damn the man, he even had her mixing her metaphors! But after all, he *had* saved her the price of a cab... and if he could share her bed without making a pass surely there was little danger of his attempting anything over a cup of coffee.

'Well——' her tone was grudging '—I *was* going to make myself a small pot. I hope you don't mind decaff.' Besides, she reflected, with some judiciously posed questions she just might squeeze him into a corner—not literally, of course; that was the last thing she wanted to do!—so that he would be forced to confess his involvement with the lovely Laura.

'All right to park here?' he asked.

'No, there's a fifteen-minute limit in front of the apartment. There's visitor parking round the back of the building, though.'

After he'd parked, they walked around to the front entrance, and while Kathryn was unlocking the main door she murmured, 'By the way, that day you came here when I was sick—how did you get in? You didn't buzz.'

'No, I didn't buzz. I had the feeling—which was later proved correct—that if I did I wouldn't get over the front doorstep. I know the manager—Jeff Bretton. He used to do janitorial work at the *Clarion.*'

'Of course. Jeff.' Just wait till next time she saw good old Jeff, she told herself irritably— he'd know what it felt like to get the sharp edge of her tongue.

'How long have you lived here?' Rex cupped her elbow as they crossed to the lift.

'Let me see—it'll be three years come July.'

'And before that?' Pushing the button, Rex leaned against the wall and looked down at her as they waited for the lift to descend to the main floor.

'Before that I lived in Halifax.'

'Alone?'

'With my parents for a while.' Kathryn met his gaze steadily. 'And before that with Derek.'

'Ah.' The lift whined to a stop at their level, and the door glided open, but before Rex stepped back to let Kathryn move past him she saw his lips tighten, saw a look in his eyes that she'd never seen there before. If she hadn't known better, she'd have thought it was a flash of…jealousy. Absurd, of course, that he would feel jealous of her relationship with Derek;

apart from the fact that it was long since over, Rex Panther had a woman of his own.

And when she slid him a quick glance as they walked together along the corridor, the expression in his eyes was as bland as it had been when he'd asked her if he could park outside the building...bland, and friendly...but nothing more, and she told herself she must have been mistaken.

Once inside her apartment, she moved around the living-room, switching on the lamps, and then, with a casual gesture, said, 'Sit down and make yourself at home. I'll be with you in a minute.'

Throwing her jacket over one of the chairs in the small dining area, she went through to the kitchen. 'Put on the TV if you like,' she called, 'or —— Oh!' A little gasp escaped her as she turned and found him right beside her in the tiny kitchenette. 'I didn't realise you were there...'

He grasped her by the upper arms and pulled her towards him. Before she had time to even guess what he had in mind, he'd pulled her hard up against him, and with one hand cupped around the back of her head he angled his face so that it was aligned with hers, and, without giving her even a second to catch her breath, he kissed her.

It was a firm kiss, a possessive kiss, and a passionate kiss. It seemed, in Kathryn's whirling mind, to last forever, becoming more and more sensual, more bone-melting, more plundering, by the minute. When at last he released her, he said, in a tone of immense satisfaction, 'That, my dear Kate, is something I've been aching to do all evening.'

Kathryn fell weakly back against the edge of the sink, glad of its support. 'I'll give you credit for one thing,' she gasped, and swallowed hard in a vain effort to relieve the tightness from her throat. 'You sure have some nerve!'

'It doesn't take nerve for a man to kiss a woman when that man knows the woman's willing.' His lips—those lips which a second ago had been working such magic on her own—were slanted in a sensual smile. A smile that set fireworks sizzling in her heart.

'I haven't said one single thing tonight to encourage you to kiss me!' If only he would move back...just a little...so that she was out of the range of those heady vibrations that were wreaking havoc on her determination to seem detached.

'No, you haven't. On the contrary, you've gone out of your way to demonstrate how reluctant you are to be in my company...'

'Then why —— ?'

'To paraphrase Shakespeare, "The lady did protest too much, methought".'

He was right, of course. She had given herself away.

'Why, Kate?' He slid his hands into his pockets and looked down at her with a frown. 'Why fight it? Whatever it is that's been going on between us——'

'There's nothing going on between us.' Kathryn turned from him, and, taking the coffee-pot from the coffee-maker, began filling it with cold water from the tap. 'Maybe I did get carried away on the island, just a little, but you can blame that on the sun and the scenery and the——'

'There was no sun while we were in the pool, Kate. And there was no scenery. Just the pale darkness before the dawn. But it started way before that—it started when I kissed you at your party in January.'

She made a little sound of protest as he took the coffee-pot from her and placed it on the countertop.

'Listen to me, Kate. I've a confession to make. Up until that kiss, I thought you were a very cool and lovely lady, but I refused to admit to myself that I was attracted to you. I've always looked for warmth in a woman...'

To Kathryn's horror, she felt tears pricking the back of her eyes. She blinked furiously and they went away. 'Thank you very much for those few kind words...'

'Hear me out, Kate.' His eyes were so serious that she regretted her flippant words. 'The day of your party, when I came into Ken's office and saw you there, looking as untouchable as if you were encased in a block of ice, something came over me—God knows what!—but I was suddenly overcome by this blinding urge to take you in my arms and kiss you till every chip of that ice melted, kiss you till your legs buckled under you.' His laugh was self-deprecatory. 'It backfired. I was the one who was left weak at the knees. But you disappeared before I could talk to you, just like Cinderella at the ball. And next day, as you know, I had to fly to the Middle East.' He reached out, and ran a gentle hand over the glossy upsweep of her chignon. 'I could think of nothing, during those two months, but the feel of your soft lips yielding under mine...'

Kathryn felt herself sliding helplessly down into the quicksand of her own desire. A rope, she thought desperately; I need a rope to pull me out of here, before it's too late...

'That person——' her voice had a choking sound '——the one you had dinner with last night—didn't you think of her at all?'

'Laura?' His strong hands now framed her face; his breath teased her heated skin. 'Yes, I thought of her, often. After all, she's my——'

'She's your woman.' Kathryn couldn't bear to look at him, afraid to see his eyes become furtive, as he came up with some lie.

A firm finger tilted her chin, forcing her to raise her eyes. There was nothing but honesty in his... nothing, that was, except a gently teasing twinkle.

'She's my sister. She's a year older than I am, and very happily married—to one of Vancouver's top realtors. She and Bob have three delightful children, and Laura has her own antique business on South Granville. She's a very busy lady—too busy sometimes—and so when I'm in town I make a point of taking her out for dinner as often as I can, to give her a break. I owe her a lot.' He cleared his throat. 'And if you hadn't darted away last night, in such an all-fired hurry, and almost getting yourself run down in the process, I'd have introduced the two of you. But in the meantime, now that we have that cleared up...'

His lips tasted as sweet as manna from heaven. Sweet, and seductive, and already so dearly familiar, they unravelled all the tight knots in the fabric of her defence. With a sigh that came from the deepest part of her soul, she yielded to him. She put her arms around his neck; she twined her fingers in the thick glory of his hair. She didn't protest as he swept her up off the floor as easily as if they were part of a dream ... didn't protest as he carried her across to the bedroom with a force of purpose and energy in every long, athletic stride. His jaw was slightly rough and he slid a kiss across her cheek, his scent musky and erotic as she brushed her lips across the smooth skin of his neck just above his collar.

And his eyes were dark with desire as he laid her on the bed and sat down beside her.

'Before we ... make love —— ' his voice was husky '——there's something I want to ask you.'

With a great, soaring joy, Kathryn knew, as if she could see into his mind—and into his heart—what that something was. He was going to ask her to marry him.

But the joy hadn't reached its peak before it spiralled down, down, down, to a dark place where Kathryn didn't want to look. She couldn't marry this man. This man who was so crazy about children. This man who wanted a family...

And she couldn't even let him propose.

He wasn't like Derek; he was an honourable man. He would never turn his back on her because she wasn't a whole woman. But she couldn't let him make the sacrifice she knew he would make, couldn't because she couldn't bear to see the light go out of his eyes as life deprived him of what he wanted most in the world.

Children of his own.

But neither could she deprive herself of this one chance to be happy. This one chance. This one night.

Tomorrow she would tell him the truth. Tell him before he proposed . . . stop him from proposing . . . and thus save him the pain of being torn in two.

'And I,' she said softly, reaching up to him, 'have something to tell you. But tonight isn't the time for talking, the time for questions, or the time for confessions. Tonight is for us.

'Tonight is for love.'

He hesitated for only a moment, but when she looped her arms around his neck and pulled him down beside her, her lips searching eagerly for his, she knew she had won.

She had managed to postpone the agony she would have to endure.

She had managed to postpone it till tomorrow.

*　　*　　*

'Now —— ' Rex gathered up their empty coffee-cups from the park bench on which they were sitting '—let's walk ... and let's talk.'

As he moved across to the rubbish container beyond the fountain, Kathryn hid a reluctant sigh and got up from the sheltered wooden bench. It had been Rex's idea to drive over to West Vancouver, buy muffins, cheese and fruit, and mugs of take-out coffee, and have an al-fresco breakfast.

He had been up before her; she'd been in such a deep sleep that she hadn't even heard him in the shower. And he had been so casual when he'd come through from the bathroom in his briefs and found her getting out of bed—a hurriedly snatched-up sheet doing little to hide her nakedness—as if sleeping with her had been the most natural thing in the world.

'Good morning, Kate.' He'd hauled her into his arms, his warm smile scattering any doubts that he might have regretted their night together. 'Now get yourself showered and dressed; it's a glorious morning, and I'm going to take you to one of my favourite spots.'

He'd kissed her then, a kiss that demanded everything—and gave everything. A kiss that was a promise ... and a kiss that was a pledge of commitment. A kiss that said, with a single-mindedness of purpose that set her mind reeling, I'm yours... and I know you're mine. We were meant for each other. I will never let you go...

Now, as Kathryn stood on the interlocking brick path leading from the fountain to the sea-walk, she felt her heart ache, felt regret like an unbearable burden on her shoulders. Last night had been a mistake. It should never have happened. Because she had surrendered to her overpowering desire to spend one night in his arms, she had done irrevocable damage to the shell she had so carefully constructed around herself. And now that the shell was beyond repair, her heart was without defence. If she could have turned him away last night, perhaps she would have saved herself this agony...

Her passion, she knew now, had had its price.

She forced a smile as he took her hand and, swinging it by his side, led her towards the sea-walk. The ocean was slate-blue and choppy, the sky denim-blue with a bank of clouds to the south, suspended over the city across the inlet. Half a dozen grain ships lay anchored in the bay, and Kathryn could see several white-sailed yachts in the distance.

'Look——' Rex pointed to a huge rock at the water's edge '——a blue heron.'

Together they watched as the elegant bird rose gracelessly into the air and glided away, just above the surface of the water. Seagulls wheeled and screamed above, and, below, dozens of surf scoters and American wigeons bobbed and dipped on the rippling waves. The air was rich with the scent of salt and seaweed, and spiced by the fragrance drifting from the broom that blazed like sunshine in the flowerbeds lining one side of the sea-walk. Spring had come early, and daffodils, tulips and bluebells made a splashy show of colour. Even as she admired them, Kathryn spared a thought for her parents on the east coast; Halifax, she had heard on the morning news, had during the night been struck by one of the worst blizzards of the winter.

'Kate——' Rex's voice broke into her thoughts, his tone as velvet-soft as a caress '——let's walk out to the end of the pier, where we can be alone. As I said last night, I have something I want to ask you——'

'And I——' Kathryn quickly brought her focus back to the man at her side, as she interrupted him before he could go further '——have something I want to tell you. May I...go first?' She looked up at him as she spoke, and surprised a look of such adoration and wonderment on his face that she almost cried out.

'With your hair loose like that ——' he cap-
tured the long strands dancing in the wind and,
ignoring passers-by, brought them to his lips,
his gaze ensnaring hers so she couldn't look
away '—you look like a sea nymph. Golden,
mysterious, seductive...'

With every word he spoke, he was only
making things more difficult for her; she
wanted to call out, Stop! but she didn't.
Instead, she just smiled—a wan smile, she was
sure—and fell in with his step as he led her to
the pier.

They walked to the end without talking, and
then sat down on a wooden bench, with their
backs to the wind. Rex made to put his arm
around her, but when she involuntarily pulled
away slightly he just laid his arm along the back
of the bench, not touching her.

'I want to tell you about myself
and...Derek,' she said. 'About our relationship, and why we broke up —— '

But before she could go any further, Rex
broke in with a quietly spoken 'That's not
necessary, Kate. Whatever there was between
you and Derek, it's over. You don't owe me
any explanations—what happened in the past
is your own business. I know all I need to know
about you —— '

'I want to tell you what happened between us.' Kathryn's voice was equally quiet, but very determined. Rex must have detected that note of steely resolve, because he said no more.

'Derek and I met when I was in my last year at university—he was one of my lecturers. Though he was several years older than I was, and an exceptionally talented photographer, he liked my work and took me under his wing. But what started as a platonic friendship changed within a few months to something different—something serious—and he proposed to me.' Kathryn bit her lip. 'I was in love with him, or I thought I was... but when we became engaged my parents asked me to wait a year before getting married. They seemed to have some reservations about him. Anyway, I reluctantly agreed to wait...'

As she faltered, Rex said softly, 'You don't have to go on, Kate, if it's too painful.'

She looked down at her hands, which were folded together in her lap. 'After the year was up, my mother and I began to make plans for the wedding. But then one night I became ill. I... began haemorrhaging... badly. I was hospitalised.' Kathryn took in a deep breath and closed her eyes. 'The gynaecologist found... large fibroid tumours in my uterus. Benign... but nevertheless... and there were other problems too. He told me he would have to remove my uterus.'

He didn't touch her. But his 'Oh, my God, Kate' had so much compassion, so much love in it, that she felt a pain in her throat as the muscles tightened.

'So they operated, and removed it.'

They took it away and left her a shell.

The wind had risen while she was talking; now it lifted her hair and she felt it whipping around her cheeks. Her hands were cold as a corpse's as she raised them and pulled the strands back from her face. 'So of course, I can't have children.' She tried to talk lightly, but her words sounded tinny and insubstantial. 'And Derek...no longer wanted to marry me. He said...he wanted children...of his own. And he said I wasn't the same person, not the same person he'd fallen in love with. He said...she didn't exist any more.

'So you see...' Was that her voice? She felt so numb that she couldn't believe that she was still able to talk. 'That's why I decided to put all my energies into my career. I'm not really an...Ice Woman, Rex. It's...just...there's no point wasting time crying for the moon.'

The sound of a float plane droned across the water towards them, mingling with the wail of a police siren somewhere in the distance. Rex didn't say anything...

But then—Kathryn was amazed at the feeling of calm that had settled over her now that she had said what she had to say—what could he say?

'Not many people know,' she went on, staring at the water. 'My parents, and my sister Nicole... and Derek, of course. But I thought I should tell you.' This, she knew, was going to be the hard part. She felt every muscle in her body tense; she felt every cell cringe in protest... but she knew she had to do it, knew she could do it... and with her fingers curled into her palms so tightly she almost cried out with the pain of it she forced herself to say the words that had to be said.

'Oh, I know you aren't serious about me— we're physically attracted to each other, that's all—but perhaps if we kept seeing each other... well, I know it seems presumptuous of me to think there was even the slightest chance you might find yourself beginning to fall for me... I'll never let any man get serious about me, Rex. I don't want to hurt anyone again... the way I hurt Derek. I just thought I'd let you know... right at the beginning. While we're still... just friends.'

For the longest time, he didn't make a sound. Not a word. He didn't even make the tiniest move that might have let her know he had heard. But even though they weren't touching, she could sense the tension in his body, as if it were her own.

Was he struggling to conjure up some words of sympathy, words which would convey that he felt compassion for her, but at the same time let her know subtly, but surely, that he, like Derek, saw her now in a different light?

But of course she had, by the clever manipulation of her own words, given him a clear way out.

A way he would be a fool not to take.

I'm glad you told me, Kate, she could almost hear him say. Even though we are, as you say, just friends.

Yet, despite the sorrow that seemed to be dragging her down into some dark pool of agony, she could not stop herself from posing the question that would bring the answer she didn't want to hear... the answer that would, like an early frost, kill the bud of their relationship before it ever had a chance to blossom.

'So——' her gaze was hard and bright as she finally turned to look at him '——you said you had something to ask me. What was it, Rex?'

Dear God! She would have given her soul not to have seen that expression in his eyes, not to have seen the agony of pity there, the glisten of tears. She didn't want that...didn't want anyone's pity. Least of all his.

'Yes...yes.' He shook his head, as if his brain had suddenly become addled. Standing up, he rammed his hands into the pockets of his trousers, and walked away from her to the chained railing at the edge of the pier, several yards from where she was sitting, her arms now clasped around herself as if she were in pain.

How strange, she thought. She was weeping, but there were no tears.

Frozen, shivering, she sat there...for hours, it seemed, though it couldn't have been for more than three or four minutes.

When he turned round, his face was pale and drawn, his black hair tossed into an unruly tumble...that wonderful wavy black hair that curled into the collar of his leather jacket—how could she ever have thought it too long?—and his eyes were still shining, but she knew that that could have been caused by the wind.

He came back and stood in front of her, looking down at her. 'Kate, you're right. I did say I had a question I wanted to ask you...'

As he paused, she felt as if every cell in her body was on hold. Waiting. Waiting for... what? A miracle?

'I was wondering if you'd like to come to a party with me tomorrow afternoon. At my sister's place.'

Miracles didn't happen. She should have known that.

She had given him a way out... and he had taken it. She knew that that hadn't been the question he'd been going to ask her the night before, knew it as surely as she knew now that that was a question he'd never ask.

But though she'd given him the opportunity to slip out of an awkward situation, she wanted him never to know just how much it had cost her to do so. She would never let him know that she'd guessed he'd been going to propose.

And the way to do that was to accept his invitation... let him think that yes, she believed that was the question he had been going to ask.

'I'd love to come to your party.' She somehow managed to get to her feet. 'Thanks for the invitation. And now —— ' she somehow managed a smile, though it was in all likelihood a very watery one '——I'd appreciate if you could drive me home. Saturday's my catching-up day—laundry, shopping, cleaning, and so on—and I'd like to get started.'

As they walked together to the car park, Rex seemed to be lost in thought. But when they reached the car, he turned to her, his features taut.

'Have you ever thought of adopting?' he asked quietly. 'Lots of single women do, nowadays.'

She shook her head. 'It's the right thing for some, I know...but not for me, I'm afraid.'

He paused for a moment, as if searching for the right words. 'You couldn't bring yourself to...love someone else's child?'

Didn't he realise he was subjecting her to sheer torture? 'It's not that.' She cleared her throat. 'I...I think it would be selfish...to take a child...when that child could have both a mother *and* a father.'

'Ah.' He exhaled a deep sigh. 'I see.' Then, after an endless moment, when he just stared into her eyes as if he were hypnotised, he muttered a soft exclamation and, tearing his gaze away, unlocked and opened the passenger door. But as Kate made to slip by him, to her surprise he put an arm round her and drew her close, so close that she could see every individual lash fringing his beautiful tawny eyes.

'Thank you for being so honest with me, Kate,' he murmured, and pressed a kiss on her brow. 'You were right—there were things about you I *did* need to know. I never really understood you before.'

But he understood her now.

And he understood that she was not the right woman for him, not the right woman for a man who was so crazy about children. He didn't, of course, say the words, but she could hear them echoing around in her head nevertheless.

He let her go, and she slipped into the car. It was so much warmer inside . . . yet she found herself shivering. Tomorrow she'd go to the party with him. And from now on, she would be what he would want her to be, what he would expect her to be: friendly, and casual— just two people who happened to work on the same newspaper.

And after tomorrow, they need never meet socially again.

CHAPTER TWELVE

KATHRYN hated cocktail parties with a passion.

Why on earth, she often wondered, would mature adults want to stand around for hours, drinking, eating, and making small talk? There were so many other, more enjoyable ways to entertain and be entertained. But she had let herself in for this one, and so she would just have to grin and bear it.

At least, she reflected as she parked her car in the road in front of the Cape Cod house where Rex's sister and her husband lived, it was far too cold and wet to be any place but indoors. The rain had started at dawn, and had been lashing down continuously ever since; the streets were awash, and the sky—what one could see of it—was the colour of lead. As she hurried up the path leading to the house, she noted absently that the air was dank with the smell of wet earth from the flowerbeds on either side of her.

The doorknocker was a wooden one, in the carved shape of a woodpecker. She felt herself

253

tense as she rapped it loudly; Rex would no doubt be the one to come to the door...

But she was wrong. Laura, dressed in a powder-blue blouse and matching tweed skirt, opened the door, and with a welcoming 'Hi, come away in' ushered Kathryn into a brightly lit hall and took her dripping brolly from her.

'What a day!' she continued, with a smile. 'So dark and dismal. Imagine having to have the lights on indoors at this time of year. Oh —— ' she chuckled '—I should introduce myself, shouldn't I? I'm Laura.' She dropped the brolly into an antique brass stand. 'And you, of course, are Kate. Rex talks about you all the time.'

Kathryn had been about to correct her, say her name wasn't *Kate*, but Kathryn; the other woman's eyes, however, were so friendly, and so warm, that she bit back the words. Perhaps they would be taken as a snub; and somehow, it didn't seem to matter any more. Kate, Katie or Kathryn...it wasn't important; why had she ever thought it was? 'He does?' she asked lightly, as she handed her shiny black raincoat to Laura. 'All good, I hope!'

'As a matter of fact —— ' Laura shook the raincoat before turning to hang it in the hall closet '—no.'

'*No?*'

Laura turned back to her, and with wry amusement in her voice went on, 'If he were to be believed, you're the most impossible female he's ever met!'

'Oh.' Kathryn couldn't help smiling. 'I don't think I'm really impossible... It's just that he seems to bring out the worst in me.'

Together they crossed the hall, and as they went into the drawing-room Kathryn saw that it was empty. Not only was it empty, it was rather untidy. A copy of the *Clarion* and the glossy *Weekends Wonderful* supplement had been tossed down by one of the armchairs, a cup of coffee sat steaming on an end table, and Lego was scattered on the Berber carpet, over by the bay window. The fire was almost out.

She said, with obvious dismay, 'I'm sorry— have I come early? I thought Rex said to be here at four.'

'No.' Laura crossed to the hearth, and, taking a couple of logs from a huge wicker basket, placed them on the glowing embers in the grate. Immediately, sparks caught the bark, brightening the room. 'I told him four—you're right on time.'

'But...' Kathryn's voice trailed away; how could she say what she was thinking, without sounding rude?

Laura straightened, and looked at her curiously. 'Is something wrong?'

'If I'm not early... is everybody else late?'

'Everybody else?' Laura frowned. 'I don't understand. Did Rex invite others? When he phoned yesterday, and said he'd invited you to join us today, I assumed it would be just you.'

'But... aren't you having a... cocktail party?'

'A cocktail party? Good heavens, no! If there's one thing Bob and I loathe, it's cocktail parties. No, it's Melissa's birthday party— we're going to eat when they get back. Bob and Rex have taken all the kids except little Jessica to the matinée at the Odeon—they used the station wagon and my van.' She glanced at her watch. 'They must have got held up in the traffic—they should have been here ten minutes ago. Did Rex actually say it was to be a cocktail party?'

'No,' Kathryn sighed, 'he didn't. He just said "party", and I assumed "cocktail party".'

'Are you disappointed?'

'No... no, I hate cocktail parties too.'

'Good! Oh...' Laura scooped up the glossy supplement from the carpet and flicked it open at the Flame Cantrell feature. 'Before I forget, I must compliment you on these!' She tapped the coloured pictures Kathryn had taken in and around the pool that morning at dawn. 'These photographs are absolutely marvellous. Imagine the elegant Flame Cantrell letting you snap her in her bikini with her hair dripping wet and not a scrap of make-up on—and doing a mini-Demi Moore, with that tell-tale convex curve of her tummy!' She chuckled. 'And of course Rex's piece is journalism at its best. Any other writer might have sensationalised the story, but he treated Flame's confessions with compassion and respect. Who would ever have guessed that poor woman had such an unhappy childhood...? Anyway, you and my brother are both to be congratulated.'

'Thanks, Laura. I was really pleased with the way things turned out...after a very bad start.'

'And that's putting it mildly, according to Rex!' Laura closed the magazine and dropped it on to a chair. 'Now you must be dying for a cup of hot coffee. Sit down by the fire. I'll be back in a jiffy, and we can have a chat before the children come back...because, believe me, when they do, it'll be far too noisy around here for conversation! Melissa and her friends are at the giggly stage, I'm afraid. Make yourself at home.'

A children's party. Kathryn had managed to hide her dismay while Laura chatted on about the Flame Cantrell feature, but now that she was alone she felt her shoulders slump. Why, considering what she'd told Rex yesterday, would he have invited her to a children's party? She thought she had known him better; she had given him credit for greater sensitivity than he obviously possessed. Wouldn't he realise, after having seen her distress when she'd talked about being unable to have a child, that bringing her to a children's party would be rubbing salt into the wound? She loved children, but sometimes it was more than she could bear, to be around them ...

She'd been wandering aimlessly around the room as her thoughts had tumbled around unhappily ... and now, as she came to a halt in front of the fire, she found herself staring at a photograph on the mantelpiece.

It was a photograph of two people. One was Rex—tall, dark, arrestingly handsome—and the other was a woman. Kathryn felt her heart clench as she saw the intimacy of their pose. They were standing under an apple tree that was in full blossom, and the laughter they were sharing was the laughter of two people with perfect rapport. The woman was fragile-looking, with elfin features and short black curly hair...

Kathryn felt the unfamiliar burning of jealousy.

Hardly aware of what she was doing, she took the silver-framed picture from the mantel, and stared with morbid fascination at the beautiful stranger. Stared at her high cheek-bones, at her perfect white teeth...but her eyes, which Kathryn knew would have revealed the most, were concealed by a pair of butterfly-shaped sunglasses ——

'Here we are!' Laura's cheery voice broke into her thoughts. 'Do you take cream and sugar?'

Feeling as if she'd been caught snooping, Kathryn felt her cheeks turn pink as she put the photo back on the mantelpiece and turned round. 'I take it black, thanks.' She moved across to the nearest armchair.

'That's a lovely picture, isn't it?' Laura waited till Kathryn had sat down before handing her a mug of coffee. 'The nicest one I had of Bronwyn and Rex; that was why I had it enlarged and framed.' She smiled. 'Even in school, Bronwyn was photogenic—she was always the prettiest in the class pictures.'

'Bronwyn?' Laura seemed to think she knew who the woman was. Kathryn's puzzlement was apparent in her voice.

'Oh!' Laura looked at her in astonishment over the rim of her coffee-mug. 'Rex's wife— hasn't he told you about her?' She saw immediately by the stunned look on Kathryn's face that he hadn't. 'Good heavens.'

'Rex is married?' Kathryn's voice was stiff. 'But he told me...he didn't have a wife.'

Laura hesitated for just a second, and then, putting her bone-china mug down on the table in front of her, she said, 'He doesn't have a wife, Kathryn. Bronwyn's dead.'

Kathryn jerked her hand convulsively, almost spilling her coffee. But before she could respond, she heard the sound of a child's cry.

'That's Jessica.' Laura got to her feet. 'She was up late last night, so she had to have an afternoon nap today. Kathryn...I'm sorry... I really thought you knew.'

There was such a look of concern in the other woman's eyes that Kathryn knew she ought to say something to reassure her. But what could she say? Anyway, her throat felt so tight that she probably wouldn't be able to speak...even if she had been able to come up with just the right words.

Laura hesitated again, but when the awakening child gave vent to another wailing cry she said, 'I'll have to go to Jessica. I'm sorry, Kate.'

As she left the room, Kathryn slumped back in her chair. What a mistake she had made in coming here; Laura obviously thought that there was far more between herself and Rex than there really was. And only now did Kathryn realise that she knew absolutely nothing about the man. She had slept with him, she had given herself to him, she had opened up her soul to him by telling him her secret.

He had always teased her about being withdrawn and reserved ... but *he* was the one who hadn't been open. Yes, he must find it heart-wrenching to think about his late wife, and it must indeed be a cause of great sorrow to him. But he could have told her he'd been married.

She put her coffee-mug on the end table by her armchair and got to her feet.

She would leave now. When Laura came back into the room, she would make some excuse, tell her she wasn't feeling well ... anything. But she had to get out of here ... and she had to get out before Rex came back.

She didn't hear footsteps, because of the thick wall-to-wall carpeting in the hall, so the first intimation that anyone was coming was the faint creak of the door being pushed open. It would be Laura.

Kathryn inhaled a deep, calming breath, and turned to face the door. Silently, she rehearsed her words. Laura, she would say, I've got this dreadful, pounding headache. Will you excuse me if I leave...?

The door opened wide...to reveal Rex.

'Hi,' he said quietly as he came in. 'Forgive me for being late. We got caught up in a horrendous traffic jam on the way home. I should have been here to greet you—and I meant to——'

'That's all right.' He had never looked so heart-breakingly attractive, Kathryn thought; he was wearing a silver-grey cashmere turtle-neck and a pair of black jeans that accentuated the length of his legs, the powerful muscles of his thighs. Was he still in love with his wife? she wondered tormentedly. Had he been thinking of Bronwyn when he had been making love with her? Oh, she had never known such pain existed as was tearing at her now. She had to get out of here, before she gave herself away. Ice Woman. That was how he'd thought of her, in those days before he had kissed her; and that was how she wanted him to think of her now. 'I was just about to tell Laura I'm leaving,' she said in as light a tone as she could muster. 'I'm not feeling too well. I shouldn't have come out this afternoon, but —— '

'Laura talked to me just now when I came in. I'm sorry,' he said, and she saw an expression of regret in his eyes, realised he knew she had just fabricated an excuse to leave. 'I'm sorry she told you about Bronwyn. I was —— '

'That has nothing to do with why I'm leaving —— '

'I was going to tell you myself, this afternoon.' He went on as if he hadn't heard her. 'I meant to steal some time with you alone, before the party —— '

'Why didn't you tell me it was your niece's birthday party?' Ice Woman? She almost laughed. It was impossible for her to conceal the agony she was feeling; it was obvious in every word she uttered. 'How could you have tricked me this w —— ?'

'Oh, God.' He sighed heavily, and raked his hands helplessly through his thick dark hair. 'I've gone about this all wrong, haven't I? Kate, believe me, the last thing in the world that I want to do is hurt you —— '

'Kate, Rex is back——' Laura's voice preceded her into the room '——but I don't know where he's gone... Oh, you're in here!' Her worried features relaxed into a smile. She walked across to her brother. 'Bob has taken all the kids down to the family room. He's going to play some games with them—keep them down in the basement, while I cook the hamburgers.' She grimaced apologetically. 'You'll have about fifteen minutes alone before all hell breaks loose! OK?'

'Thanks, Laura.' Rex put an affectionate arm around his sister. 'I appreciate it.'

Laura gave him a quick peck on the jaw, and then she left, clicking the door firmly behind her as she went out.

'Rex——' Kathryn started towards the door '——I want to go home.'

He caught her arm as she would have passed him. 'Yesterday, when you wanted to tell me about Derek, I listened, Kate.'

She froze, as if she were caught in a trap. He didn't say any more... but he didn't have to. He was right; he hadn't wanted to listen to what she wanted to tell him about her relationship with Derek, but he had given her that courtesy. Wasn't it only fair that she should do the same?

Feeling every cell in her body shrink from what she was about to hear, she nodded, avoiding his eyes. 'All right.'

'Sit down, won't you?'

She moved to the couch, and sat down, perching on the edge of the middle cushion.

He began pacing the room, his hands in his pockets; he was restless, Kathryn knew... She could hear the clinking of keys or coins as he played with them.

'Bronwyn Sellars and I were friends all the way through high school,' he said. 'We were never sweethearts, just friends...very close friends. She confided in me when her romances went awry...and I in turn confided in her when things went wrong in my own life. We studied together at times, and we played a lot of tennis together when our own friends were otherwise occupied. We had the kind of boy-girl platonic relationship that is enduring and steadfast.' He paused by the window, and stood there, looking out, his back to Kathryn. 'We both attended UBC, but after we graduated we went our separate ways. Bronwyn began her own lingerie design and manufacturing business here in Vancouver, and I landed a job with a newspaper in New York. We corresponded by letter, and by phone ... but for years, because of our different schedules, we didn't see each other.

'Then one Christmas Bronwyn came to New York on a marketing trip. It was wonderful being together again ... It was as if we'd never been apart. And so—foolishly, as it turned out—we asked ourselves why we couldn't have the whole ball of wax. We were already closer than most of the married couples we knew, so we decided we wanted even more of our relationship.'

He turned round slowly, and his eyes locked with Kathryn's. 'We decided to have sex.'

'Rex, I don't want to hear this.' Kathryn started to get up. 'It's none of my business——'

'Sit down, Kate.' Rex's voice was grim ... so grim that she found herself doing exactly as he said. 'I'm not finished.'

She sank back against the cushions, feeling as spineless as a jellyfish. 'All right,' she whispered. 'Go on.'

'We slept together. It should have been great—we both *wanted* it to be great—but it didn't work out.' His brow furrowed, as if he was still trying to explain that to himself. 'It just didn't work out. God knows why—the spark just wasn't there. Did we try too hard?

Did we expect too much?' He shook his head. 'Or perhaps it was just that we were so damned comfortable with each other as friends that it was...almost embarrassing...to become intimate—physically.'

'But you married her.' The words blurted from Kathryn without any conscious volition on her part; she'd become so engrossed in what he was saying that she'd forgotten herself.

'Yes, we got married. You see, a couple of ——'

The door burst open, and Rex broke off as a little girl with long blonde hair came into the room. Kathryn immediately recognised her as the youngest of Laura's three children. Last time she'd seen her, she'd been dressed in a turquoise and pink snowsuit and pink snowboots. Today she was wearing a floral dress, and a pair of white lace tights that outlined a pair of straight, sturdy legs. Her chubby cheeks were flushed, as if she'd just awakened from a deep sleep, and there was a drowsy look in her eyes. Eyes that were the dreamy blue of a robin's egg. Eyes that were fringed with dark blonde lashes...eyes that turned first to Kathryn. After staring unblinkingly for several long seconds at the stranger on the couch, with a tiny frown puckering her brow, the little girl then shifted

her glance to Rex. Having sought some re-
assurance from him, and received it by way of
a soft 'Hi, Jess' and an encouraging grin, she
murmured something unintelligible, and made
for the Lego scattered on the carpet by the bay
window.

The child was everything Kathryn had ever
dreamed about. Her long hair—the colour of
summer sunshine—was pulled back in two
bunches, with errant strands spiking from the
back of her neck and over her forehead. The
fingers curled around the Lego were dimpled,
her nose was tip-tilted, and her skin looked as
smoothly textured as the finest silk. And her
little body was plump but firm, just made for
cuddling.

'She's adorable.' As the whisper escaped
Kathryn's lips, she felt a bright flame of colour
stain her cheeks. Dear God, had she no self-
control? No pride? The naked hunger in her
voice brought a wave of shame sweeping over
her, so intense that she could almost feel herself
drowning in it. Such raw wanting was too per-
sonal to be displayed before another; such desperation of the soul could only serve to
embarrass the listener...and embarrass him
deeply. Kathryn felt as if every last remnant of
her shell had just fallen away—the shell that

was herself—and exposed to the world something that should never have been revealed.

Fighting the sob that had started to rise in her throat, she pushed herself to her feet. She couldn't look at Rex—couldn't face the expression of pity she was sure would be in his eyes. One day he would surely have children of his own...and in the meantime he lived just down the street from his sister and her family of three; he could spend all the time he wanted with Melissa, Jessica and their brother. He could never understand the agony that was now tearing at her.

'I've got to go.' Her voice was thick with tears. 'Please don't stop me...'

But once again, he stepped in her way. Grasping her shoulders with his hands in a grip that was so tense that it almost hurt, he held her away from him just far enough so that he could see right into the depths of her eyes.

'You're in love with me, aren't you, Kate?'

It wasn't a question; it was a statement, and spoken with a quiet conviction that left Kathryn no room to lie.

And what would be the point, anyway? He knew the truth.

'Yes.' She closed her eyes so he wouldn't see her pain. 'Yes, dammit, I'm in love with you.'

Her humiliation now was complete.

She felt his grip tremble, heard him exhale a shuddering sigh. 'Oh, my darling Kate, you'll never know just how afraid I was that I was wrong.'

The day had already drained away much of her inner strength. The courage she'd had to dredge up to come to the party in the first place, the shock that had rocked her when she'd discovered that Rex had once been married, the leaden feeling of disappointment she'd experienced on realising he'd kept such a vital part of himself a secret from her—all had combined to weaken her normally stout core of resilience. Now, dazed and dizzy, as she listened to Rex's huskily spoken words she couldn't seem to make sense of them. He was *afraid he'd been wrong*? What did that mean? He *wanted* her to be in love with him? But...

Feather-light kisses brushed her eyelids.

'Don't hide from me, Kate.' One warm hand slid to cup her jaw, the fingertips touching the sensitive skin below her ear, the pad of his thumb gently skimming her cheek, removing the trace of a tear. 'Please.'

Raising her eyelids was probably the hardest thing she'd ever had to do. But, feeling as if he'd hypnotised her with the velvety persuasion of his voice, she tried. She could feel her eye-lashes fluttering, could feel a nerve flicker in her cheek. But when, finally, she looked up, and saw the love shining there, joy—so intense that it was almost a pain—seared her heart as if he'd branded it with a white-hot branding iron, branded her with his name.

And even as she reeled, mentally, the wonder of it just too much for her, he put his arm around her and drew her across the room to where the child was playing.

'Jess,' he said softly. 'There's someone I want you to meet.'

The little girl looked up at Rex and smiled her innocent, enchanting smile. Releasing Kathryn, he reached down and scooped the plump toddler up into his arms. The chubby hands disappeared round his neck, one pink cheek nuzzled against his silver-grey cashmere sweater.

'Say "Hi" to Kate, Jess,' he coaxed.

'Hi, Kate,' she murmured sweetly. Her blue eyes were dreamy and accepting.

Rex put his arm around Kathryn again, holding her even closer this time—so close that she could feel the strong, steady beat of his heart against her shoulder. 'Kate, darling——' affection, pride, happiness—all these and more were in his voice as he spoke '—I'd like you to meet Jessica, the very special little lady in my life.' He dropped a kiss on the top of Kathryn's head before capturing her eyes with his own as he added, with a slow, lazy smile that had her heart turning over, 'She's my daughter, Kate.'

It was hours later before Kathryn and Rex were able to steal any time alone together, because Bob had come in at that very moment to announce that the party was under way.

It was years since Kathryn had been to a children's party... and Melissa's might have been the best, or the worst, in history; she would never know. She seemed to float right through it in a haze.

'I know I've done everything back to front,' Rex had whispered wryly, as Bob swept them through to the dining-room, 'and I know I've a helluva lot of explaining to do. But Kathryn, my darling, you will marry me, won't you?'

There was no need for her to say a word; the answer was in her eyes, shining there for him— and all the rest of the world—to see.

Finally, though, the party was over. The guests had gone home, and the children were all in bed—Jessica too; she was sleeping over at her aunt Laura's, as she always did on Sunday nights. 'I drive her to daycare in the morning, on my way to work,' Laura explained, as a blissful Kathryn helped tuck the little girl in. 'She's used to the routine, so even when Rex is at home we stick to it.'

'Can you give me a drive home, Ms Ashby?' Rex's voice was teasing. 'I didn't bring my car.'

'Yes, of course.' Try as she would, Kathryn just couldn't stop smiling. 'I'll drop you off.'

They both thanked Laura and Bob for the party, and Kathryn could see by Laura's expression that she knew everything between them was just the way she wanted it to be. She gave Kathryn a tight hug as she bade her goodbye.

'Welcome to the family,' she whispered. 'And come back soon.'

The rain had stopped, and the evening had turned mild.

'You should walk home,' Kathryn suggested. 'Instead of cadging a drive from me. It would do you good. Perhaps walk off some of the pounds you put on this afternoon. How many slices of birthday cake did you have? Was it three?'

'Four...but who's counting?' Rex chuckled, as he got into the passenger seat.

Before Kathryn could start the car, he put his arms round her and pulled her into a breath-taking embrace. 'You didn't answer my question, you know.'

'What question was that?' His face was light and dark, planed and shadowed by the slanting rays of the street-lamp; she thought she might just die from love.

'Besom!' he growled. 'Drive me home and come in for a nightcap. I'll ask you the question again.'

She didn't answer till she'd driven the short distance along the street to his house; sweeping her car up the drive, she parked, and sat back. 'Thanks for the offer,' she said primly. 'But you know . . . I don't drink and drive.'

'Who said anything about driving?'

She jerked her head round and stared at him. 'Just what are you suggesting, Mr Panther?' she asked.

He reached over and took her keys out of the ignition. As she gasped in mock-indignation, he pocketed them. 'You're my prisoner,' he said firmly. 'Until such time as I decide to let you go.' With that, he leaned towards her and kissed her again, slowly, lingeringly, as if he couldn't bear to drag his lips from hers. Kathryn felt exactly the same way.

He kissed her again as they walked to the front door, he kissed her before he unlocked it, and then again, after he'd opened it. And once inside, he shut the door, and, trapping her between his arms as she leaned back weakly against the wall, he pressed his hands against the wall, at either side of her head, and kissed her again in the dark.

Finally, he groaned, and with one last passionate brushing of his lips across hers he pulled away. She heard a click, and the lights went on.

'Come through to the kitchen,' he said, his voice husky, 'and let's make a pot of coffee. And not decaff. I intend getting not one wink of sleep tonight.'

She must be dreaming, Kathryn thought, as she floated through to the kitchen, hand in hand with this man she loved. It couldn't be happening like this...

'How do you like the house?' He slanted her a quizzical look as he took a jar of coffee from the fridge. 'I hope you do...like it, I mean. But if you don't, we can look for something else. I bought this one because it was handy for Laura's. God knows how I'd have managed without her to look after Jess. I coped for a while in New York, with a nanny, but it was constant chaos.'

Kathryn began to feel as if she were slipping off the cloud on which she'd been floating; and reality began to make itself felt again. 'Rex...' She leaned back against the countertop for support. 'I feel...I feel as if...you're rushing me.'

He stared at her unblinkingly for a long moment, as if he'd just noticed her, and then he blew out a sigh. 'Kate, I'm sorry.' He made a helpless gesture with his hands. 'It's just that...I've never done this before. I've never been in love before——'

'No, I don't mean that. What I mean is...I think we have to talk. There's so much I don't understand.'

Rex plugged in the coffee-maker and took one of her hands in his. 'I know you were puzzled when you found out Jess was my daughter, because I'd said Laura and Bob had three children and you assumed those were the three you saw that morning we went to the airport——'

'No, I know now that they have an older son who's at boarding-school on Vancouver Island. That's not what's puzzling me.' She looked around the large kitchen. 'May I...sit down?'

She smiled ruefully. 'I must admit I've never felt like this before either—nobody ever told me love made a woman feel woozy!'

Rex dragged her across to the kitchen table, and, pulling out one of the Windsor chairs and turning it round, sat down on it and settled her on his lap. Between kisses, he murmured, 'So, my darling, what is it you want to know?'

'How can I think...how can I concentrate...with your lips at my throat?' she complained breathlessly. 'Can you exercise some control...if only for a minute or so?'

'Sorry.' He took his arms from around her waist, and, leaning back, supported himself with his elbows on the table. 'Fire away.'

Kathryn bit her lip. 'On Friday night...before we made love...you said you had a question you wanted to ask me.' She felt her cheeks turn warm but forced herself to go on. 'I...thought you were going to propose, but —— '

His eyes darkened. 'Kate, I was going to...though I hadn't intended to —— ' He frowned as she made a tiny sound of dismay. 'Just hear me out, Kate. I had to consider Jess. She's been my whole life, since Bronwyn's death—she's been everything to me. What you'd said in the past—that there was no place for children in your future —— '

'Because I couldn't have any,' Kathryn said in a quiet voice.

'But I didn't know that on Friday night.' He looked at her for a long moment. 'On the island,' he said finally, 'when you said you didn't like shells, I wondered —— '

'Ever since I found out I couldn't have children, I've felt empty, just like —— '

'Just like a shell. I finally figured that out, yesterday, when you told me...about your surgery.' As he spoke, he reached behind to a shelf on the wall, which she hadn't noticed; on it was a display of shells. From it he took a conch—it looked rather like the one he'd found on the beach, that second day on the island. 'Take it, Kate. Hold it to your ear, and listen. Really listen, this time.'

His fingers touched hers as, slowly, she took it. She held it, hesitating, her eyes fixed on his, uncertainly. He nodded, and, taking in a breath, she wrapped her hand around the shell, and held it against her ear.

Closing her eyes, she listened.

At first, what she heard was just the rustle of her hair as it brushed against the surface of the shell. But then...almost immediately after ... she heard it ... the sound of the surf. The echoing rush of water, creaming on the beach. Musical, magical, it lured her into wanting to hear more. She concentrated, holding her breath, and as she strained to listen she saw, against the black backdrop of her closed eyelids, the sun shimmering on the bleached white sand, the sky streaked with pink and yellow, the Caribbean waters blue-green and clear; and then she thought she heard sea-birds cry, and the breeze sighing through the palm fronds, was sure she could smell the sweet fragrance of the tropical flowers ...

'You're smiling, Kate.'

She felt his fingers curve over hers, and she let him draw the shell from her ear.

'You know now—don't you, my darling?—about the music and beauty of the soul. I believe that everything on this earth, everything God made, has a soul. And you, Kate Ashby ——' he put his arms around her and pressed his cheek to hers '——have the most beautiful soul in the world.'

Kathryn knew she would have been happy to sit there for the rest of her life, on Rex's knee, with the whisper of his voice in her ear, murmuring words of love that made her heart sing ...

But she still had some questions to ask.

'Rex...' A long time later, breathless and flushed, she drew away from him. 'Why did you marry Bronwyn? If you weren't in love with each other.'

She saw a deep sadness in his eyes. 'Haven't you guessed? A couple of months after her trip to New York, Bronwyn found out she was pregnant.'

At last she understood. Kathryn made a little sound of sympathy, and Rex went on,

'We both, of course, wanted her to have the child. She was as crazy about kids as I was. And then...the natural solution seemed to be for us to marry. For the baby's sake.' His smile was wry. 'Maybe not the wisest decision in the long term, because it was on the cards that one day one of us might fall in love and want out of the marriage. But we'd both reached the grand old age of thirty-two without that having happened, so...' He shrugged, as if to say, We had nothing to lose.

'How...did she die?' Kathryn had hesitated even as she framed the words in her head, but decided in the end that it would be best to find out everything she wanted to know now, so there would be no niggling, unanswered questions in the back of her mind.

'She was murdered.'

Kathryn stared at him in speechless horror as he went on in a flat voice, 'She was in a department store one afternoon three years ago—just a few months after Jess was born—when a man burst in with a gun and fired a series of shots at random. He killed six people. Bronwyn was one of them. They found out later that he was a disgruntled ex-employee of the store. He turned the gun on himself when the police caught up with him.'

'Oh, Rex ...'

Rex's arms tightened around Kathryn. 'I had to get out of New York, Kate. Too many memories. I've come to terms with what happened, but for the longest time I couldn't even speak about it.' He smoothed a hand over her brow, soothingly. 'That's why I kept my home life private—didn't discuss it with any of the people at the *Clarion*. If they'd known I'd been married, had a child, they'd have asked about my wife ... and—'

'Oh, Rex, I'm so sorry.'

'Bronwyn and I were happy together ... I have no regrets. It's almost three years since her death; it's time for me to put the past where it belongs.' He slid Kathryn off his lap, and as she stood up he got to his feet beside her. 'And as for the future... I intend arranging my life so I spend less time abroad, and more time at home...'

'Charlie said he'd heard that the lady in your life was complaining that she didn't see enough of you...?'

He grinned. 'Charlie was right. Jess likes to have me around, Kate...'

'Jess is a female after my own heart.' Kathryn twined her arms around his neck. 'Just one more question, and I promise you it'll be my last. You said you had been determined not to propose to me, that night when you stayed over at my place...?'

She didn't need to finish the question. 'You swept me off my feet, Kate... and if you hadn't pulled me down beside you and kissed me I would have. But I hadn't meant to. I had meant all along to wait till... after you'd met Jess. I needed to see you with my daughter first, Kate... not that I really had any doubts. But I needed to be sure in my heart that you would love her, the way I love her. Anything less wouldn't do. And when I saw the way you looked at her...'

'Oh, Rex, I was bleeding inside, humiliated and filled with despair, because I knew I'd revealed my Achilles' heel, my yearning to have a daughter just like Jessica.' Kathryn shook her head, her eyes shining with tears of joy. ' "God moves in a mysterious way, His wonders to perform." '

'He does indeed, my darling Kate,' Rex murmured as he lowered his lips to hers. 'He does indeed.'

MILLS & BOON NOW PUBLISH
EIGHT LARGE PRINT TITLES A MONTH.
THESE ARE THE EIGHT NEW TITLES
FOR MAY 1994

———————— * ————————

UNWILLING MISTRESS
by Lindsay Armstrong

ORIGINAL SIN
by Rosalie Ash

ISLAND OF SHELLS
by Grace Green

A TAXING AFFAIR
by Victoria Gordon

WOUNDS OF PASSION
by Charlotte Lamb

SUDDEN FIRE
by Elizabeth Oldfield

LOST IN LOVE
by Michelle Reid

MAKING MAGIC
by Karen Van Der Zee

MILLS & BOON NOW PUBLISH
EIGHT LARGE PRINT TITLES A MONTH.
THESE ARE THE EIGHT NEW TITLES
FOR JUNE 1994

———————— * ————————

BITTER HONEY
by Helen Brooks

THE POWER OF LOVE
by Rosemary Hammond

HEART-THROB FOR HIRE
by Miranda Lee

A SECRET REBELLION
by Anne Mather

THE CRUELLEST LIE
by Susan Napier

THE AWAKENED HEART
by Betty Neels

ITALIAN INVADER
by Jessica Steele

A RECKLESS ATTRACTION
by Kay Thorpe